Peace Weavers

Had he seen the brooch? Back in her pocket now, it felt warm to her fingers. And her face was burning. He was staring at her, and she was staring at him. Why couldn't she move? It was as if they were held together by invisible bonds. Something passed overhead though whether it was a bird or a jet she couldn't have said. Then another voice broke the spell.

"Don't you two want to see what we've found next door?"

Hilde wrenched her head round to see Beth and a crowd of people round the other trench. When had they turned up?

"It's very exciting. Come and see." Beth turned back to the trench behind them.

"Wanna hand?" Friedman offered his.

"NO!" She clambered out, but not before their fingers had touched and her pulse rate tripled.

Other Titles by Julia Jarman

Point

Peace Weavers

Julia Jarman

SCHOLASTIC

Scholastic Children's Books,
Euston House, 24 Eversholt Street,
London, NW1 1DB, UK
A division of Scholastic Ltd
London ~ New York ~ Toronto ~ Sydney ~ Auckland
Mexico City ~ New Delhi ~ Hong Kong

First published in the UK by Andersen Press Limited, 2004
This edition published by Scholastic Ltd, 2006

10 digit ISBN 0 439 97771 1
13 digit ISBN 978 0 439 97771 5

Printed and bound by Nørhaven Paperback A/S, Denmark

2 3 4 5 6 7 8 9 10

To Annie and Caitlin,

and all future Peace Weavers

Acknowledgements

My thanks are due to Rebecca Garrill and to Suffolk County Council Archaeology Service; to Jo Caruth, Senior Project Officer, for taking me on a dig and sharing her expertise; to Alan Baxter, manager of West Stow, where I first found the brooch; to Kathleen Herbert for her inspiring book *Peace-Weavers and Shield-Maidens* (Anglo-Saxon Books, 1997); to Liz Jansch for advice on base life and first taking me to Stow; to Lee Weatherly for advice on all things American and much more; to the girls of Wolverhampton High School; to friends, family and members of the other SAS – you know who you are! – and to my editors, Audrey Adams and Jane Harris, for their encouragement and helpful suggestions.

The lines from 'Stopping By Woods On A Snowy Evening' from *The Poetry of Robert Frost*, edited by Edward Connery Lathem, published by Jonathan Cape, are reprinted by permission of The Random House Group Ltd.

Before Words

My story begins in northern Europe fifteen hundred years ago, when a young woman sailed across the sea to "peace weave" between two warring tribes. She landed in England in what is now Suffolk, where another strand of my story takes place – in the twenty-first century. War is again an issue, for a modern young woman, since the region has become home to a United States Air Force base. In March 2003 planes flew from this base to attack Iraq, provoking a debate – that still goes on – about the legality, the morality and the practical consequences of that war. An archaeological dig, a piece of jewellery and an unusual idea, link the two strands of my story.

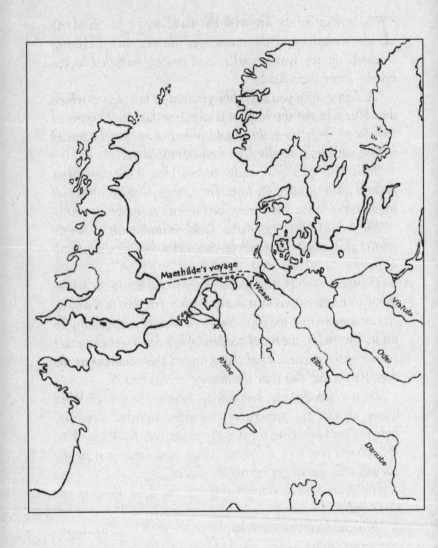

Maethilde's voyage

*T*he girl sat by the fire with the jewellery in her hand. As she looked up at the messenger, flames cast flickering shadows on the wattle walls, and smoke spiralled to the beams above their heads.

"A sleeve clasp you say?" She glanced at her sleeve, which was blue like the sky roof on a summer day, then again at the clasp. There were three gold pieces, each one engraved with a pattern of scrolls. 'But how does it work?'

'It is one of a pair, lady. Sleeve clasps are the latest fashion in the land of my lord. The square pieces join the cuff edges at the wrist. The three-sided brooch is for ornament.'

The brooch was exquisite. Gold inlaid with a single garnet gleamed in the firelight. She had never seen anything so fine.

The messenger took the other clasp to the doorway, where the girl's mother stood by a loom, catching the last of the light. As the woman took the clasp she glanced at her daughter with pride. The red in the braid borders of her dress was the exact colour of the garnets. Had she conjured this moment as she dyed the thread? But now the mother chided herself.

'Be not proud, lady. You did not choose the colour. Wyrd alone weaves the pattern of our lives together, crossing, twisting and breaking the threads as she sees fit. Wyrd chose the colours and shot the shuttle back and forth, just as she carried this messenger across the waves."

The evening sun slanted through the door, lighting the girl's red-gold hair.

"Maethilde, if you keep the clasps, we shall need to unpick the sleeve seams."

"May it please the gods that your daughter keeps them," said the messenger. "They are a pledge of troth and peace between our two peoples."

"Two peoples now," said the mother, "though one before."

She didn't say — before your lord's fathers left this land to fetch food for their kin, and never came back from the island on the other side of the North Sea. Anglia some called it and others Engleland.

"And could be one again," said the messenger, and didn't add — if your weapon-men would stop raiding my lord's lands for food which is not theirs. He didn't ask where the father was now or the sons.

"Engles both, we from the mainland, you from the island, we should be friends not foe," said the mother.

"That is my lord's wish too."

The girl kept quiet, letting her mother weave words with the messenger as the shuttle clicked back and forth.

"Maethilde's father is an Engle, I a Saxon. Our wedding brought peace to our tribes."

"My lord is a New Engle, his wife-man a Mercian. Their wedding brought peace to their tribes."

"A wedding is a weaving, and now your lord..."

"Wishes that your daughter should wed his son — to weave peace between Old Engle and New. He has heard of her word-wisdom and her cheerful heart."

There were more treasures in the casket at Maethilde's feet — rings and brooches and goblets of copper and bronze, and combs of walrus tusk for her hair, but the gold clasps set with garnets were what won her heart. She had never seen anything so comely and surely there was meaning there for eyes to read? For was not that a face hidden among the curved lines, of a deer hiding in tangled branches?

A deer for my dear?

My hart for your heart?

Was that the message from her would-be husband?

"Who sent my daughter these gifts?"

"My lord, though the clasps she seems to like so well are from Manfried, his son. They are his special gift from him to her."

My lord, Manfried. My lady Maethilde. The girl sounded the words in her head.

The mother said, "He must be a fine young man to choose so sweet a gift."

Manfried and Maethilde.

Maethilde and Manfried. They went well together.

"He made the gift himself, my lady."

The mother raised a brow. "I trust he bears a sword as surely as he bears a goldsmith's file?"

"He lacks no desirable asset, lady — or will not he says — if he may have your daughter's hand."

"A word-weaver too?" The mother turned to her daughter. "Maethilde must have her say. She is fourteen years old, but it is no small thing to leave the hall of her kinsmen and cross the sea to weave peace between our lands."

No small thing indeed, for words could make peace or break it, and in some hearts old hatreds died hard. It would not be *easy living in another hall, finding words to turn loathing to love. But the girl had no doubts. She would weave peace as surely as she would weave the cloth to clothe her family. So she stood up — and up — till her red-gold curls brushed the roof beam. The messenger, tall like all the Engles, had never seen a girl so tall.*

"Tell Manfried, I accept his gifts." Her voice was husky but clear. Her eyes, blue as the bluebell woods in springtime, shone as she spoke. "Tell him I will come as Peace Weaver to his hall."

"You will plight your troth before the Earth Mother?" said the mother.

"I will," said the girl, "today, for it is Freya's day and that is good."

Chapter 1

Friday, not the 13th but it felt like it. Hunched in the back of the car, Hilde covered her ears as the jets took off in V formation. Ugly mottled creatures with sweptback wings, farting filth and flames, their engines screaming as they scored the sky with thick black lines.

"Those F-15s heading for the Gulf, Dad?" Tom was in the front being matey with Frank. Dad! Tom's dark hair – like their mum's – flopped forward as he nodded towards the vanishing aircraft. Don't think of Mum.

"Yeah." Frank nodded. "Putting pressure on Saddam the Insane."

Hilde eyed the back of Frank's head. Why was she ginger like him?

Angrily she read the board at the roadside as the stink of kerosene seeped into the car.

1

UNITED STATES AIR FORCE
WHISTON RAF BASE.
PRIVATE PROPERTY.
STRICTLY NO ENTRANCE WITHOUT PRIOR CONSENT.

SHOW IDENTITY AND WAIT FOR CLEARANCE

That's what they'd been doing for ten minutes, waiting to get permission to enter a foreign airbase on British land!

"Sorry, kids." Frank Browne's fingers drummed the dashboard as the barrier ahead rose and fell once more. "Used to drive straight through – before 9/11."

Silence. Tom bowed his head reverentially. Frank looked tense as well he might. If he thought she was going to act lovey-dovey just because he'd started playing daddy, he was very wrong. She noted the razor wire on the perimeter fence, the watchtowers disappearing into the distance, spiking the dreary, flat as a pancake landscape. Home sweet home. More jets took off, blackening the sky, which had been half decent, blue and white as if it were a summer day, not a freezing cold one in January. Now she noticed a cluster of white spheres near the horizon.

"Radomes," said Frank, who must be spying on her in the rear view mirror. "Golf balls, the locals call them. They detect incoming aircraft."

"In case of invasion." Tom nodded sagely.

"No no!" Frank was quick to correct. "Invaders

would be spotted way before they got this far. Those things help guide our own aircraft."

"Haven't we been invaded already?"

Tom glared at her. "You're sounding like Mum, Hild."

"So?"

But she wished he hadn't mentioned their mother. How could she, how could she, a pacifist for heaven's sake, have sent them to live here? With an American father they hardly knew, while she...But best not to think about what she was doing. Dangerously near tears, Hilde focused on a weed thrusting its head through the wire, half expecting a soldier to yell at it to get back inside, but the military were busy up the road checking vehicles. She ought to try and see exactly what they were doing.

"Increased alert. Sorry, kids, since..." But more jets drowned Frank's words.

Hilde guessed what they were. Frank put on a CD and closed his eyes as a soprano screeched – till Tom nudged him a few minutes later. "Moving, Dad."

There was only a white van between them and the barrier now, and two soldiers were moving in on it.

"Are those M16 carbines?" Tom was showing off.

"Think so. Oh no. This is gonna take longer."

Most drivers had been allowed to stay in their cars, but White Van Man was getting out. A heavily armed soldier was taking him to the guardhouse, just outside the barrier, and another was opening the van's tailgates. A black labrador jumped inside.

"Why choose him for a going-over?" Tom wondered aloud.

"Why not?" said Frank. "Anyone of them could be a terrorist."

"Looks like a painter and decorator."

"Could have Semtex in his paint cans."

"And you expect us to live here?" Hilde snapped at Frank's reflection, saw him open his mouth, and think better of it. Good. Then he got out of the car to talk to someone in the truck behind and Tom attacked.

"Why are you so negative? Mum's gone and that's that – without you. Accept it. And she asked Frank to have us – remember? While she went to Scotland to stop the war. Ha ha ha."

If only she were in Scotland.

"At least she's trying to stop a bloody war! And he left, for your information, though you're too young to remember."

"At least Frank's got a house and a decent car."

Maeve – their mum preferred Maeve to Mum – had a caravan and a beaten-up Volvo.

"You care about these things?"

"So do you, hypocrite. You've been longing for a mobile and I didn't hear you turn down Frank's offer to get you one. Living on base is gonna be great. You'd know if you hadn't refused all his invites."

Tom had come back from weekends with Frank full of it. He said living on base was like going to America once you got groundside – as opposed to airside where

4

munitions were kept. He'd come back with all the jargon too. Shops, no stores, movies – everything was American, even the currency. His mates had been dead impressed with the gear he'd brought back – jeans half the price of British ones and better quality. He'd supplied half the school.

"Frank's OK," he insisted. "Pity about his job – but you ought to like that – and his music, but think positive," he laughed. "We'll get him a headset!"

She didn't answer and he switched to his favourite topic, the brilliant sports facilities on base. And how he'd played American football when he was here, and proved to be good. Was he really as unworried as he seemed? What would he say if he knew where their mum had really gone?

As White Van Man moved onto the base Frank got back into the car and drove up to the barrier. No one had opened the paint cans, she noticed. So much for high security. But she wished she hadn't rowed with Tom. Wished she were more like him in some ways. Wished she didn't care or know so much. It was stressing her out. Now a black soldier in camouflage gear was peering in at Tom, who straightened up. Was he going to salute? On the other side Frank was showing his ID to a white girl soldier who stared into the back at Hilde.

"My two kids," Frank said. "They're coming to live on base."

"They got ID?"

"Not yet."

Frank pulled into the side, and they all piled out and into the guardhouse, where Frank told everyone their business again. Guardhouse. She expected bars, but it was just a reception area with a counter. One wall was covered with cutesie posters with uplifting messages. Another had a huge TV showing American football.

"Look this way," said a pasty-faced boy soldier and flash – their photos were taken, by a tiny camera on the end of what looked like an angle poise lamp. Maeve would have gone mad about invasion of privacy. He hadn't even asked. Seconds later, Pasty Face was handing them ID cards with shots of their faces.

"Excuse me," she managed to say. "You didn't…" But then Tom nudged her, and nodded towards a poster of an eagle flying high. DARE TO SOAR it urged. YOUR ATTITUDE DETERMINES YOUR ALTITUDE IN LIFE.

"So?"

But Tom didn't answer. An officer in airforce blue had just walked in and was talking to Frank. Tom joined them and Frank made introductions.

"Lieutenant-Colonel Karl van Jennions, my son Tom and…" He nodded in her direction. "My daughter, Hilde."

"Hi, Tom. Hi, Hilde. And it's just Karl, OK?" He took off his cap and folded it up. "I'm off duty. Tom, didn't you play American football with my boy Friedman when you were here last? And weren't you pretty good? He'll be real glad to see you. He's trying to

6

get a team together, doing a bit of coaching in fact, but a lotta American kids are more into soccer now. I'll give him a buzz. What's your address now, Frank? I guess you've changed billet."

Hilde listened as Frank said yes, he'd moved from single to family quarters, but Tom seemed tongue-tied. Hilde guessed why. Hero worship. The officer was everything he admired, tall, dark and good-looking in an obvious sort of way – and he probably dropped bombs on people. And – it was clear from the conversation – he knew Frank as the base librarian. So Tom's little secret was out. He wouldn't be able to pretend his dad was a fighter pilot as he had back at Crosby Upper. He didn't know that she knew that.

Tom recovered when they were on their own again, driving into the residential area. Just like America? Well it wasn't exactly Hollywood, or New York. It looked more like an English council estate in fact, with an out-of-town shopping centre attached. The sight of a McDonalds next to a KFC next to a Pizzahut revived Tom's spirits, but he went into shock again, when they stopped for traffic lights by a motor pool where residents were filling their gas-guzzling cars. But it was the building site next to it which upset him.

"What are they doing? That's where the football field was!"

"Yeah, but don't worry." Frank was reassuring. "There's another field near the Junior High. And that's

7

not a building site, by the way, not yet, though it's gonna be another accommodation block. But right now it's a dig." He looked to see if Tom had understood. "Those guys in hard hats, they're archaeologists, hoping to find an Anglo-Saxon cemetery. See how they've stripped and levelled the surface. Might even have started digging. Excuse me?" He leaned across Tom. "Yeah. See that trench near the sidewalk? Might be an old grave!"

Hilde watched Tom trying to look interested. Frank sounded like those hairy men in jumpers who got excited about bits of old pot. An old grave – so what? There'd be tons of new ones if the war with Iraq went ahead. If? More planes screamed overhead and she couldn't help thinking about Maeve. The date for war was obviously in someone's diary. Maeve was kidding herself if she thought she and her Quaker friends were going to stop it. Those F-15s carried bombs. She'd sat outside enough airfields herself to know that.

Deep in thought, she didn't notice the lights change. Didn't notice Frank driving on, or that he'd pulled up in front of a house – till she saw his pale face peering into the car through the rear door.

"Hilde honey, we're here." He sounded as if he was in a crummy sit com. "You were miles away. Here, pass me your bag."

"Thanks. I'll carry it myself."

Tom was already halfway up the concrete path of 281B Washington Street, the middle house in a block of three. It was the last in a long line of identical blocks, on the corner with another street, which looked just the same. Frank said they'd soon get the hang of the layout. It was a grid system and all the roads were named after American presidents.

Hilde followed Tom to the grey front door. Even when it was closed you could hear the whine of aircraft. Outside smelled of kerosene. Inside smelled of fresh paint.

Frank showed them the ground floor – entrance hall, kitchen-diner and lounge, not much bigger than Maeve's caravan, and all very beige. "Just one thing, kids," Frank hesitated at the foot of the stairs. "It's probably best to keep quiet here, about what your mom's doing."

And he thought she was sitting outside a submarine base in Scotland, making her usual protest against war and nuclear weapons.

Hilde carried her bag upstairs. One bag. She hadn't brought much stuff because she didn't intend to stay long. As soon as her best friend Ruthie got back from the school skiing trip, she was going to go and stay with her.

"My own room? Great!" Tom flung open the door with his name and a picture of an American footballer on it. Hers had a nameplate but no picture, because Frank Browne hadn't seen her since she was five, so he'd had no idea what she was like. But, she smiled as she lugged her bag into the bedroom, he was beginning to find out.

9

Chapter 2

Ducking to miss the low beams in the sitting room of Pyghtle Cottage, Karl van Jennions kissed Marty his wife, hugged his daughters and friendly-punched his son. Then he sank into a chair and began to pull off his boots.

"Guess who I saw today," he said to no one in particular.

"Madonna?" said Olivia.

"Britney?" said Cally.

"Sorry, not pop stars." Karl laughed as the girls wandered into the kitchen after their mother. He told Friedman about meeting Frank Browne.

"Didya know his boy's coming to live on base – and his daughter? Tall girl. Never even knew he had a daughter. Wasn't Tom a good player? Well, if I were you, son, I'd get right back on base and sign him up for football before the soccer lot get him." He glanced at his watch. "Give you a lift if you like."

"Thanks, Dad, I'll go first thing in the morning." Friedman suppressed a mock salute. He wasn't in his dad's squad yet. Then he put another log on the fire and watched the sparks fly up the chimney. His dad watched from the other side of the inglenook, and Friedman wondered what he was thinking. How he'd hate to leave Pyghtle Cottage where they'd lived for the last two years? Their days there were numbered. They'd be moving back on base as soon as the new accommodation block was ready, for added security the Pentagon said.

His mom had sighed when they got the news. "We're in the military so we do as we're told." His dad had never questioned the decision. But would they really be safer from terrorists on a military base than in a sleepy English village? 9/11. In his mind's eye Friedman saw the twin towers falling. Who'd have thought the fall-out would reach this far?

Next morning he found Frank Browne's place easily enough and reached for the bell. But "Hi..." died on his lips as the door opened and a grey cat shot through his legs. Not that he saw much of the cat. First, long bare legs then words on the t-shirt in front of him had his full attention. DROP DEAD. DROP DEAD rose and fell.

Friedman wasn't usually lost for words, or fazed by

girls – and this was a girl, that was clear, it was because, because… He struggled to regain his calm for suddenly his pulse was racing. But only seconds before he'd been priding himself for running three miles no sweat and now he was steaming. Because he was surprised, that was it, he realised with relief! He'd been expecting to see Tom Browne, a kid who came up to his chest, not this g-girl looking down at him.

"Yes?" Hilde was cold and the perv had been staring at her boobs far too long.

A second before Hilde spoke, Friedman raised his eyes to meet eyes the colour of English bluebells.

"Yes?" she snapped again. Why didn't he speak or go?

Because he was transfixed by the figure before him. F-figure was the word. Friedman was annoyed that ordinary words were causing him consternation. He was a sophomore, for heaven's sake, not a brainless kid. And girls weren't an alien species as some guys seemed to think. Stupid guys. Girls were human beings not, not objects. He knew, liked lots of them. So why couldn't he speak to this one?

"Yes-s?" Hilde wanted to close the door. It was winter. "What do you want?"

Fortunately Tom chose that moment to appear.

"Hi, Tom!"

"Hi…!" The two high-fived madly and the perv – she didn't catch his name – mentioned football.

As Tom dived back inside to get his kit, Hilde noted

the bag at her feet. FRIEDMAN K VAN JENNIONS III. Must be the bomber's son. She glanced at his red face. "Fried man. That fits."

Then she went back upstairs, leaving him open mouthed, and Tom reappeared. What a dumbo. She watched them from her bedroom window, walking down the street, dark heads together. Well, not quite together, Dumbo was taller so he had to bend his a bit, but they looked like brothers. Tom would like that, a big brother looking out for him, instead of a grumpy sister. She hadn't been charming, but at least she'd pre-empted the usual opening remarks. What's it like up there? Can you hear me, or shall I try my mobile?

As Friedman walked along the sidewalk with Tom he estimated that the boy was at least three grades lower and maybe eight inches shorter than he was – and that Hilde might be the same grade and not really taller than he was. It just seemed that way because she'd been standing on the step above him. That was why he'd seemed to be staring at her DROP DEADs too long. And she'd noticed. He knew she had. That's why she'd looked at him as if he were a perv. And he'd acted like a perv. Staring. Now he carried on a nearly normal conversation with Tom – about the football league – while wondering how he could see Hilde again and make a better impression. Would she be coming to Whiston High? Why did he want to make a better impression? Because he'd never seen eyes that kind of blue before? Fried man. He should have laughed and introduced himself. 'Freedman van Jennions.' Why hadn't he? No wonder she'd looked down on him, literally. She sure was tall.

"Sorry I didn't call last night, Tom." Good. Mouth and brain were functioning again. "I was watching *A Midsummer Night's Dream*." He'd liked it, liked Shakespeare, on film and stage anyway. He wasn't a redneck.

"That's OK," Tom shrugged. "Probably wouldn't have heard if you had. The house was full of neighbours giving us a welcome party."

Hilde had no idea of the effect she'd had and certainly hadn't intended. She'd only gone to the door because Frank's cat had pestered to go out. She hadn't heard the bell, didn't expect anyone to be there, and was still wearing the baggy t-shirt she slept in. And even if she'd known Fried Man was there she wouldn't have done a Ruthie-style lightning makeover. She didn't need 'guys' as Ruthie called them.

Hilde showered, pulled on a t-shirt and a pair of combats and stowed the rest of her stuff in the so-called 'closet', a tiny walk-in cupboard. What now? She caught sight of herself in the mirror on the door, and thought it was probably as well she couldn't go round to Ruthie's. If you've got it flaunt it, Hilde. Get something that fits. Ruthie didn't believe that being six foot one repelled every male in sight, or that Hilde didn't mind.

Ruthie was five foot with boyfriends of six foot two.

"So why not vice versa, Hild? It's your prejudice that stop things happening."

"I don't want things "happening"."

"I know loads of guys who fancy you, or would if they could get near."

"By climbing up my hair, you mean? Sorry, mine grows sideways!"

"Hild, think positive. Fight the NATS! Your hair is beautiful!"

NATS equalled Negative Automatic Thoughts. Ruthie was into psycho-speak. She wanted to be a psychiatrist and favoured a proactive approach. So why wasn't she here? Frank's so-called music was doing her head in. Opera! As something yearning and very high soared up from below, she grabbed the plan of the base he'd given her. Shopping therapy. That's what she needed. Ruthie was all for that. Shops – where were they? She needed something to hold back her hair which had ballooned since her shower this morning.

Frank appeared from the lounge as she opened the front door. "Honey, where you off to?"

I'm a person not a sandwich spread! But she just pretended not to hear as she slammed the door shut.

"Hi, Hilde, how ya doing? Cold east wind. Straight from the Russian steppes. Bet you didn't know that." Sergeant Veasey came out of the house next door at exactly the same time, but made straight for his car thank goodness.

Now she felt cold and very exposed. There was nothing between his house and Frank's, nothing between any of the houses. No privacy at all. No gardens with hedges or fences, just grass and concrete paths.

As he drove away she set off, remembering the night before. The Veaseys had led the welcome committee, apologising for the absence of their kids, who had been sent home to their grandparents in the States, because both parents were about to be deployed to the Gulf. She'd made a mental note to tell Maeve about that – when Maeve got in touch. Hank and Nancy Veasey were going to set up sanitation units for the military. Translation – build bogs for the forces establishing themselves in the Gulf. Did anyone need more proof that war was imminent?

But last night was party time. Hank and Nancy had come bearing cakes. Tom had gone mad for Nancy's Peanut Butter Cookies, and she'd told him he was 'cute' and a 'real American boy just like Hank junior'. Americans were so friendly it was tiring, but what would they say if they knew about Maeve? Thinking about her when you were walking briskly wasn't so bad. They'd probably bug Frank's place, if it weren't bugged already. Now she noted the hum of overhead wires and the CCTV camera to her left on the ten-foot fence beside her. What had Maeve said? "Observe all you can especially about security. It could be useful." So what was the four-storey concrete building behind the fence? The prison? She consulted the plan. No, it was Whiston High School! But, she consulted the map again, the Base Exchange, or BX, a shopping mall, was only a couple of blocks away.

"Slides?" The assistant in the drugstore – wasn't that the same as chemist? – didn't understand.

"To hold back my hair."

She meant barettes it seemed, and yes, they had a selection, but she needed dollars as well as a new language to buy them.

As she left the drugstore her mum's words came into her head. *"Americans live in a world of their own, Hilde. It's an all-American world. Even those who live over here live in America. Some of them never step off base."*

"So why send me to live on one? I want to go with you."

"Sorry, Hilde, not this time."

"Let me stay at home then. I can look after myself."

"Not in the eyes of the law you can't."

"You disobey the law when you want to."

Once, before she'd had children, Maeve had cut through the fence surrounding a base, and got sent to prison. Hilde loved that story. Maeve was so brave.

"Only laws I don't agree with. And I do agree parents should look after their children."

"Look after me then!" It had blurted out, and Maeve had looked hurt, but three days later – after a few phone calls to Frank – she had gone. It had all happened so suddenly. Now shame and self-pity and fear welled up again as she strode along the road. What if Maeve didn't come back? Did she think she might not? Was that why she'd sent them to live with their father?

"Watch out!" A brawny hand grabbed hers. Through blurry eyes she saw a man in front of her.

Chapter 3

"Sorry about that, but..." Brawny Arm nodded towards a woman unloading a pick-up at the side of the road. He had to be an archaeologist. He had the complete outfit, facial hair, hairy jumper and yokel accent. Somehow she'd reached the dig-site they'd passed the previous day.

"It's OK," she snapped more at herself than him. "Thanks," she even managed. He'd saved her from bruised knees if not worse. Crashing into the woman's wheelbarrow would have been painful.

"Sort of thing I do all the time," laughed the woman, who didn't look clumsy at all, but brisk and efficient in yellow hardhat and checked shirt. She stuck out a weathered hand. "Beth Stansfield, county archaeologist, in charge of the site. And you?"

"Hilde, Hilde Webster." She preferred her mother's surname.

"Hi, Hilde, meet Sid, your knight in shining armour and my right-hand man. Are you really OK?" She appraised Hilde and suddenly looked hopeful. "You weren't coming to help, were you? We need all the volunteers we can get."

And before Hilde could say no, she was saying they'd only got six volunteers and three professionals and they'd only got eight weeks to excavate the whole site before the builders moved in. But Hilde would have to fill in a form, she said, if she did want to help. Sid laughed as she dived into a portacabin with OFFICE on the door.

Glancing round Hilde wondered how to make a quick exit. The work looked boring and dirty, not her scene at all. People were scratching away at the soil, some with hoes but most were on their knees. The mechanical digger she'd seen yesterday was parked in a corner,

"At least you've come properly dressed," burred Sid. "Though you might be a bit chilly, but we could lend you a jacket. Some girls turn up dressed for a fashion parade. It's all the TV programmes, making archaeology seem glamorous. Not that it ain't exciting. If you find summat, you'll be 'ooked. Won't she?" he said to Beth, who reappeared hatless now, clutching a printed form.

She gave it to Hilde with one hand, and raked her

brown curly hair with the other. "I'm afraid you've got to get this filled in before you can start. It's a Conditions of Service form. Has to be signed by a parent or guardian – if you're under eighteen? For insurance mostly. Have you got far to go? Do you live on base?" She waited for Hilde to be chatty and answer her questions.

Yes. No. Yes. But she couldn't be bothered to say so. They probably thought she was older than she was – it often happened – and neither of them seemed to have noticed she hadn't actually said she was volunteering, but it didn't matter. She'd just take the form and not come back. That was simpler than telling them stuff. That's what she intended as she muttered goodbye a few moments later.

But as soon as she rang the bell of 281B Washington Street – she hadn't got a key – Frank appeared.

"Good timing, honey." He led the way to the kitchen. "Coffee? A couple of buddies are coming round soon to have a chat about school. They're part of the school's system for welcoming new arrivals." He filled the kettle.

"No thanks," she said in a flash, "I'm off to the dig."

"Couldn't you hang on a few minutes?"

"No, and you might as well know, I'm not going to school. Not here, because I'm not going to salute the American flag every morning."

Silence. Maeve said he was wet as dishwater. She

handed him the form which he studied and signed, but then put on a shelf above the work surface, saying he was real glad she was getting involved in the dig.

"But you'll need something for lunch, honey." He started to fill plastic containers with salad stuff. "And we will have to talk about school later. Shall I tell the girls you'll be in tonight?"

"Tell them what you like!" She grabbed the food and the form and scarpered, marvelling that she, Hilde Webster, had just committed to spend the rest of the day digging in the dirt. It was deeply sad.

Later that morning, Beth enthused as she demonstrated a technique Hilde would need – scraping with a bricklayer's trowel. Beth enthused, rather like Maeve, Hilde thought, though about different things, but, unlike Maeve, she didn't seem bothered when Hilde didn't enthuse back.

"Just hope it doesn't rain." As the archaeologist crouched in a shallow trench behind the office shed, she kept glancing at the sky where cloud was building up. The wind had dropped.

"Rain's the last thing we need. We're so short of time. We've made good progress so far, marking out the site. That's what all the criss-crossed blue tape is for. But now the real work begins. Here, you have a go now." She handed Hilde the trowel. "Whiston's been an airfield since World War II. That's why we're so keen to dig here. If we do find a cemetery, the skeletons will be intact, not shattered as they'd be on farmland. Modern ploughs are a menace because they go so deep."

She watched for a few minutes.

"Hilde, that's good. You've got the hang of it really quickly. Just keep scraping away, not digging, that's important and watch out for a change in the soil colour, texture, anything. If you notice a change, stop and give me a shout, because anything you find must be recorded here." Then, picking up a clipboard with a squared plan of the trench on it, she strode off, leaving Hilde alone.

Scraping was mind numbing, not interesting at all, and yet she had to concentrate, so couldn't think about other things. Beth had said she wasn't likely to find actual bones, because the yellowy soil was mostly sand, and sand was acid, which made bones dissolve. Dissolved bones. Yuk. Why were they so keen to find them?

"Why are you so keen to find a cemetery?" Another volunteer voiced Hilde's thoughts during lunch break, when they were picnicking on the floor of another portacabin. "Wouldn't evidence of living people – like pots or buildings – be more useful than dead bodies?"

"No." Beth laughed. "Skeletons are great, full of info. They can tell you lots about how a person lived and died of course, with or without grave goods. But," she got to her feet, "so far no one's found anything on this site, and no one will if we all sit here gassing."

"Slave driver!" someone called out but no one lingered.

Back in her trench, Hilde thought about how easily other people talked. Why couldn't she chat away like them? Because she was afraid of saying the wrong thing? Sometimes. But mostly the words simply wouldn't come, or come out. They stayed inside. Trapped. A couple of men had gone to sit in their cars, but most people spent the lunch break talking. Beth had introduced her to some of them, including the other professional, a middle-aged Norwegian woman with a blonde plait, called Meri. She'd said, "How did you get interested in archaeology?"

Well what could she say to that? But now she didn't have to say anything. It was very quiet in fact. All she could hear was the scritch-scratch of scraping tools, cars going by, and occasionally the sound of a wheelbarrow being pushed to the spoil pile. They were lucky, someone said during lunch, it was a rare non-flying day so jets weren't bursting their eardrums. When they were flying overhead you needed earplugs. Exactly. Hilde remembered the day before.

It was half three exactly – she'd just glanced at her watch as she stretched to ease the cramp in her shins – when there was a shout from a trench in the far corner near the road.

"Come and see, 'ilde." Sid came over to get her. When they arrived, Beth was crouched by the trench where Meri was working. Beth pointed excitedly to a long brown bone. "A femur, thigh bone. Do you see what's happened? The top half of the body was buried in sand, so that's completely gone, but the legs look as if they might be preserved because they're on a layer of chalk."

She patted the ground beside her. "Get down here, all of you, and see how Meri's uncovering it. Watch carefully."

For maybe half an hour Hilde and the other volunteers watched, as a knee appeared, then, the top of a shin and a foot. The brown bones showed up well against the white chalk.

"Imagine the poor grave diggers," said Beth, "digging away with their wooden spades. It's obvious they got fed up trying to get through the chalk, and laid the bottom half of the body on top of it instead. See how the body's sloping."

"Know how they felt," Sid said. "It's hard enough digging through chalk with a metal spade."

One by one the other volunteers got up, inspired they said, as they hurried back to their trenches. Hilde went back to hers, not inspired, but wondering if she'd ever find anything. But as the afternoon wore on, and the heap of sandy soil at the edge grew higher, nothing exciting appeared, not even a change of colour, and her mind began to wander. Maeve hadn't rung or written. Perhaps as well. She would definitely think this was a waste of time. Don't think of Maeve. She hadn't heard from Ruthie either. When she'd tried ringing her mobile from the phone in Frank's house there had been no answer. A blister started in the palm of her hand.

Was this really what she wanted to be doing? As she put down her trowel a voice made her jump.

"Come on, Hilde. Didn't you hear the band playing "The Star-Spangled Banner"?" Beth was standing on the edge of the trench, silhouetted against a purple grey sky. "Yes really," she said when Hilde looked dumb. "And "God Save the Queen"?"

The wind had dropped and dark clouds were piling up behind her.

"They play both national anthems every evening at sunset, as the flags are lowered." She turned away. "Look, everyone's leaving." And everyone was, in couples and clusters. One couple was climbing onto a tandem. "Aren't East Anglian skies wonderful?"

Hilde nodded. The clouds were impressive, like a range of purple mountains outlined in gold where the sun was setting behind them.

"Just hope they don't mean rain," Beth went on. Then she reminded Hilde to put her tools away in a box in the office and headed in the direction of Sid who was standing by another trench. Hilde saw them studying the sky, their arms linked. Not just work mates then. She thought of Ruthie's last words, advice of course. *Just make one friend, Hild, and you'll be fine. You don't need loads, but you do need someone to keep you sane*. One friend. Easy, if you were Ruthie.

It was while stooping to pick up her trowel that Hilde saw something glint in the side of the trench. At first she thought it was the low winter light making the sand shine, but when she reached out to touch it, her fingertips felt something hard and smooth. A pebble? *If you find anything, anything, stop and give me a shout*. Beth's words were in her head, but she couldn't stop. It probably was just a stone. She scratched round it with her little finger, till it jutted out from the side for about a centimetre. Not a stone. It looked as if it were made of metal. *If you find anything, anything, stop*. But she carried on scratching till it fell into the palm of her hand. Jewellery of some sort, a gold coloured brooch or pendant, with three sides like a pointed leaf. She rubbed it gently with her finger, blew some loose sand away and saw a tiny red stone set in a maze of golden scrolls. It shone. The whole thing shone. It was beautiful. Shivers shot up her arm as her fingers curled round it. Was this what Sid meant when he said she'd be 'ooked? Did 'hooked' describe this feeling of excitement? *If you find something tell me so I can record it*. It had begun to rain. Beth and Sid were hurrying to the office. Thinking she'd better keep it dry, Hilde slipped the find into a pocket.

It was growing dark as the girl and her mother rowed to the island where the Earth Mother had her bower. Some said they heard Thor rumbling in the distance, angry because he wanted war, but Maethilde said the rumbling was Woden turning the tide so the messenger could hurry home and Manfried hasten to her side.

As mother and daughter pulled on the oars, a pale full moon hung in the sky, and floated on the rippling surface of the river. But in the fiery western sky the sun had not yet slipped below the earth. The omens were good, Maethilde said. Sun and Moon were both bestowing their blessings, and the Earth Mother too, for as she stepped into the bower, she felt a tingling silence.

"In your presence, Earth Mother,

I plight Manfried my troth."

She said it three times, for three was strong magic and words were spells — they made things happen — and what had happened could not unhappen. When she stepped out of the bower she and Manfried were wed, the threads of their lives twisted together, forever. Until Wyrd the Fate Weaver chose to break a thread but that — please the gods — was a long time off.

Mother and daughter rowed back to the messenger.

"Tell my lord that we are wed," said the girl. She gave him one of the clasps. "Give him this clasp as a token of my faith. Tell him that when we meet I will wear them both. I give him my heart, as he gave me his."

She wanted him to know that she understood the message of the brooch.

"Tell him that I am now his wife-man. I will prepare my bride-chest and await his swift arrival."

It was harvest time. If he were quick he could be here before winter. Very quick, and they could sail straight back to New Engleland before the cold came. Then together they would weave peace between their peoples.

But her lord did not come quickly. Winter came and went. Eosturmonth passed and so did Three-milking month when cows bulged with new life, but still her lord did not come. Moon month came.

Maethilde looked up at the summer sky, as she stood in the doorway of the sleeping house, fingering the clasp on her sleeve. But where was her lord, her clasp giver? Where was her dearest deer? Summer was here. Swallows were wheeling in the blue of the sky roof. House martins had built their mud nests beneath the thatches. Birds had flown swiftly north from lands far to the south, but her lord from the island across the North Sea had not flown swiftly to her. Nearly a year had passed since the messenger brought his gifts. What had delayed him? May it please the gods he was riding his sea-steed at this moment, urging the wind to carry him over the waves to her side.

Behind her, at the foot of her bed, her bride-chest stood ready. Had been ready for many weeks. It was carved from oak by her father, with hinges and clasps of bronze. She had packed and re-packed it many times with Manfried's gifts for her and hers for him, and her bride clothes.

One pair of thick fur boots.

One thick wool cloak to wrap round herself in winter.

Three pairs of soft kid shoes for finer weather.

Three of leather for the wet.

Three long overdresses.

Three long sleeved underdresses with sleeve seams unstitched, the latest fashion in the land of her lord. She felt the clasp again.

"A deer for my dear.

My heart for yours."

Now she murmured the words aloud.

There was finery for their homestead too — linen for the table, embroidered hangings to warm and brighten hall and sleeping house, sheets of linen and of wool for the bridal bed and a wolfskin from her father to cover them in winter.

Through the doorway she could see her father repairing the thatched roof of the weaving house, and beyond the buildings she thought she could see her brothers Edwin and Egbert, on the other side of the river, in the sheep field, on higher land beyond the cow meadow. From time to time a high-pitched whistle reached her ears, for Edwin was training two young pups — and his younger brother — to herd the sheep. The mother dog had saved many a silly sheep from getting lost and attacked by bears or wolves. There she was, the mother dog, grey and brown, looking like a wolf herself, her belly close to the ground. As Edwin whistled she circled the flock, the pups at her side copying her moves. If only all the men could be so happy working close to home.

Some of them were busy in the fields, tending stock or weeding crops, many none too keen. The more restless were hunting in the forest, for none of them had gone raiding this year. Urged by the women they had stayed at home.

"Stay this year, for greater gain next." Maethilde had heard them. "Maethilde will bring joy to her husband's hall in the New Engleland across the sea. Maethilde will peace weave then send for her kin. And till that time she will send food to us on the mainland from the more fertile soil of the island."

Much hung on her success. Here the sea was encroaching, eating up the land, leaving less for farming and hunting. But on the island there were thick forests stretching for miles and teeming with game and wild boar, and the soil in the cleared land was rich, yielding bountiful crops. If she did her work well with skilful word weaving and kind deeds, her new kin from across the sea would not let her old kin starve. Much depended on her.

"When will he come?" Now she closed her eyes and as she did she heard a shout and hoof beats. Her heart quickened. Someone, a stranger, was dismounting from a brown cob in front of the weaving house. She waited for him to turn his dear face to hers...

Chapter 4

It rained heavily on the way back from the dig. Hilde's fleece was soaking when Frank opened the door, before she rang the bell. He must have been looking out for her. Towel in hand, he was apologetic.

"Here, honey. I should have met you in the car, but thought about it too late. Haven't you got a coat? We must get you one – and a key."

"I've got a coat, thanks."

"Oh good. Er, there's something for you, on the hall table."

A postcard! From Maeve? She grabbed it as he headed back to the kitchen. But no, it wasn't from Maeve; it was an invite to a jewellery 'spree' from Nancy next door. Jewellery. She felt the thing in her pocket. Couldn't believe that she'd walked off site with it. Why hadn't she handed it in when she'd handed in her trowel?

"Are you OK, honey?" Frank stood in the kitchen doorway. She hadn't moved from the foot of the stairs. "I said is pizza and salad OK?"

"I'm vegetarian."

"Yeah. You told me. It's spinach and mozzarella."

Smart arse. "Suppose so."

As she climbed the stairs sounds of a sports channel came from Tom's room, or maybe next door or both. The walls were so thin, but not see-through she hoped, as she dived into the bathroom and locked the door. Then she emptied her pockets onto the edge of the sink.

A triangle of gold coloured metal, a bit longer than the tube of lip salve beside it, it glimmered beneath the mirror light. She turned it over dislodging some grains of sand. Was it a brooch? There was no pin but a raised bit where a pin might have been attached. And now it seemed brighter than when she found it. Carrying it in her pocket must have polished its surface. It seemed to be made of strands of metal twisted, maybe welded together. Or perhaps it was solid and engraved to look that way. The red centre glowed.

"Honey!" She jumped as Frank knocked on the door. "The pizza'll be twenty minutes!"

"OK."

She showered quickly, keen to look at it again, hold it in her hand. And it was while wiping the steamed-up mirror, that she caught sight of a face, the brooch's reflection – some sort of animal face – that seemed even clearer when she held it in the palm of her hand. For a second or two it looked abstract, a design of twists and curves, but then the stylised face appeared, a long nosed face with curly antlers, a ram's or a deer's? Yes, a deer's. It looked as if it were hiding in a thicket, antlers and branches entwined together.

A deer for my dear.

My hart for yours.

My heart for yours!

Words and pictures were in her head.

"Hilde! I need a pee!" Tom was banging on the door.

"Coming!" Slipping the brooch into her bathrobe pocket, she opened the door and dived into her own room to get dressed.

At Pyghtle Cottage Friedman let himself in, after seeing Tom Browne back to Frank Browne's place. It was dark, but there was no one at home he soon realised, and as he climbed the stairs to his room, somewhat breathless, he wondered if he was getting sick. His stamina wasn't what it should be, and hadn't been at football. He'd fumbled the ball so badly Harley, the other coach, had noticed. Had made an ass of himself in fact. Ass! Donkey? Jeez! Suddenly there was a picture in his head, from the video of *A Midsummer Night's Dream* – of a great looking girl trying to pull, like date, like make love to a donkey, because she thought it was a real cool guy.

"Let that be a lesson," his dad had laughed. "Love's blind, a madness."

"No, Karl!" his mom had protested. "That's infatuation!"

Love? Infatuation? The big question was – was Hilde Browne really drop dead gorgeous? Luckily her brother hadn't suspected anything.

"Bite your head off, did she?" Tom had said as they walked to the football field.

"Nah," he'd lied, thankful the kid couldn't see inside his head.

"Don't take it personally. She doesn't want to live here, that's all."

"What's her name?" He'd tried to sound casual.

"Hilde, with an e. Never spell it with an a. She's sore with our mom, 'cos she's done a runner. Hilde and Mom were like this," he'd gone on, meshing his fingers together. "So Hilde's taking it out on everyone else. She's fair like that."

English irony? Tough though, her mom leaving. Not that Tom seemed fazed. And kid brothers weren't the best judges of character. But Hilde Browne couldn't be beautiful, he suddenly realised. She looked like her dad. Same hair. Same white skin, as if he'd been sucked by vampires. So some kids called him Frankenstein. Then why did he keep seeing this golden vision? Why did DROP DEAD seem like a come on? Oh no! His mom and sisters were back. Better head for the bathroom and a cold shower.

35

In Washington Street, when Hilde came downstairs Tom was enthusing about Frank's cooking.

"It's just a take-away, Tom."

"At least you got it in. See, Hild, you don't have to do the cooking here or the shopping."

He was getting at Maeve again. She sat down, refusing to rise to his bait – and Frank changed the subject, to school unfortunately.

"Starts early here, 8 o'clock, and Tom, as I said, I'm sorry but you'll go to Junior High."

Tom was miffed because he couldn't go to the same school as Friedman. You didn't start High School till Year 8 in the States.

"Hilde, you'll go to High School. We'll discuss when later."

"What's to discuss?" Tom stopped eating.

Frank ploughed on. "Tom, you start Tuesday, OK? They're closed this Monday for some reason. Do you want me to take you first day?"

"No thanks. Friedman said he'd call – for us both. The schools are next to each other. So why's Hilde not going?"

Neither Frank nor Hilde answered.

After dinner Frank gave her twenty dollars to take to Nancy's spree, saying allowances were another thing they'd have to sort out.

"Maybe you could ask the other girls what they get?"

"Maybe." Part of her wanted his cash, part of her didn't. She only went because she didn't want to spend the evening thinking how she shouldn't have taken the brooch.

The Veaseys' house was a mirror image of Frank's but it looked different, mostly because the walls were covered with photos and embroidered pictures.

"My handiwork," Nancy said as she saw Hilde looking at a cross-stitched picture of a thatched cottage, on the lounge wall. "Keeps me outa trouble, I guess, and I like to think it makes for being more home-like." It was hard to think of Nancy as a soldier. She was fat and comfortable looking with bobbed fair hair.

"Y'have to do what y'can," laughed another woman. Nancy introduced her as Sindy who was running the spree, and she introduced her twin daughters.

"This is Sylvie, and this is Janey."

It was hard to tell them apart. They both had blonde ponytails and pink glittery t-shirts.

"Do you play soccer, Hilde?" said Sylvie or Janey.

"No."

"You don't?" They exchanged amazed glances. "But we thought girls' soccer was big over here. It's the latest thing in the States."

So? – she wanted to say – that doesn't mean everyone has to do it, but said instead that she wasn't sporty. Soon all the seats and floor space were covered, mostly by bums even bigger than hers, she noted with satisfaction. Then Sindy stood up in front of an enormous TV, to begin her sales pitch. Hilde soon switched off. The jewellery, mostly plastic, wasn't her style. On the screen adverts and 'The Simpsons' alternated soundlessly. She thought about the brooch thing which she'd left in the pocket of her bathrobe. Had she hung it on the door or left it on the floor? Then, suddenly it seemed, everyone was clapping and she wondered how quickly she could leave. But before she could Nancy brought in coffee and Coke and slices of yellow Pina Colada cake, and more Peanut Butter Cookies and another cake called Key Lime pie, and it seemed impossible to get away. Sindy said that if everyone bought something – though there was no obligation – Nancy would get a really cool free gift. But it was a while before the buying and selling began. As soon as she politely could Hilde bought a gold chain that she thought Ruthie would like, and left pleading tiredness. But not before she'd agreed to see Janey and Sylvie the following night. They were it seemed the 'buddies' appointed to help her settle into school.

"We'll call, OK? Then we'll go hang out at Wendy's."

She didn't ask what or who Wendy's was. Perhaps they'd told her? She just wanted to see the brooch thing. It was beginning to prey on her mind. Why had she pocketed it? She'd never done anything like that before.

It was ten o'clock but not really dark outside. Light shone from uncurtained windows. Raindrops sparkled round yellow streetlights. Aircraft lights moved in and out of clouds. She was tired after her day of manual labour. At least she hadn't lied about that, and now she felt sick too. As she waited for Frank to open the door, she decided to tell Beth in the morning, not exactly confess, just say she'd found it when they were all leaving, which was true, sort of. But then she changed her mind. She'd look like a thief. Maybe she was one, technically. There were strict rules about moving stuff, let alone taking it off site. Beth had made that clear. So it would be better to put it back where she'd found it, 'find' it again later and then tell Beth.

Frank opened the door.

"Want a night cap, honey? Chocolate?"

"No thanks." She headed upstairs.

"Buy anything nice?"

"Yes. For Ruthie, my best friend."

"Goodnight then."

"Night."

Her bathrobe was hanging on the closet door. She got the brooch thing from the pocket and held it in the pool of light beneath her bedside lamp, felt her pulse rate quicken as her fingers curled round it.

A deer for my dear.

My heart for yours.

The words were in her head again. What did they mean? In the morning she must take it back. Put it back, and then carry on digging. That thought surprised her. Was she hooked then? Surely not, but it would be good to find the owner of the brooch, and it might have been buried with a body. Grave goods.

Couldn't they tell you lots about the owner? She uncurled her fingers, took a last peep and then slipped it under her pillow to keep it safe till morning.

Maethilde looked across the greensward to the weaving shed where the rider was dismounting. Waited as he exchanged words with her father, who came down from the ladder. Waited for her first glimpse of her lord. Then he turned towards her and he was not her lord! The face was not Manfried's face, which strangely she felt she would know. But it was the messenger's face, the same messenger who had brought Manfried's wedding gifts. But now his face was paler despite the warmth of the day. What had happened? Had Wyrd the Fate Weaver changed the pattern on her loom? Had...? But she dare not complete the question in her mind.

Later, when horse and messenger had been fed and watered, mother, daughter and messenger met in the hall, as they had at harvest time, nearly a year ago. But now there was no flickering fire in the central hearth, and the messenger's words came slowly. She heard him say she could keep the marriage gifts for it was no fault of hers.

"What is no fault of hers?" Her mother spoke for Maethilde could not. Her mouth was dry, her lips frozen. A chill ran through her veins, though the sun was creeping through the door.

Her lord, his lord he said, could not marry her.

"Why not?" the mother asked.

"Because he has married his stepmother."

"His stepmother! But why?"

"Because his father wished it, arranged it before he died," said the messenger. "Not long after I returned from delivering the wedding gifts, Manfried's father heard the raven call his name, meaning he had but thirty days to live. Fearing war between his wife's people and his own tribe, he ordered Manfried to wed himself to his stepmother to keep the peace between Mercian and Engle. Thirty days later he met his death."

"But he was — is — wed to me!" Maethilde stood up — and up. The messenger thought she had grown even taller. "He was forsworn and the stepmother was still wed to his father!"

"The young man agreed to this?" asked the mother.

"To keep the peace between Mercian and Engle."

"And what of the peace between Engle and Engle?" said the mother.

"There is a sea between Old Engle and New," said the messenger. "Trouble from Mercia seemed more likely."

But father and son and stepmother had reckoned without Maethilde. "What of my good name and Manfried's? We are wed. A wedding is a weaving. We are bound. He gave his word and he cannot break it."

"They both gave their word," said the mother. "What has happened cannot unhappen."

"Maethilde may keep his gifts, lady. She will be rich."

Maethilde's eyes blazed. "What are riches without honour? Tell the stepmother she must go!"

"Word weave, daughter, peace weave." The mother laid her hand on Maethilde's arm.

"If words can mend this matter, I will use them." Maethilde turned to the messenger. "Tell your lord if he will not come to me, I will come to him to peace weave in his hall. But if he will not have me as Peace Weaver I will come as Shield Maiden and fight for what is right! My good name is more precious than his gifts."

Chapter 5

Hilde was in the middle of a dream.

Word weave, daughter. Peace weave.

"If words can mend this matter." Strange words were in her head. She was arguing with her mum. No – she tried to hold the dream in her head – not her mum. Maeve didn't talk like that and she never wore dresses. Big Ben boomed up from below … Prime Minister … French betrayal … liberation of Iraq… The dream slid away as she waited for an explosion. "Liberation my backside! Hilde, did you hear that?" But Maeve stayed strangely quiet and the newsreader carried on. If Saddam Hussein … does not reveal the whereabouts of his Weapons of Mass Destruction he will have to accept the serious consequences, the President told Congress yesterday. Awake now, she realised where she was.

Frank must be listening to the BBC news.

Fleetingly her dream returned. A blue dress. The girl in her dream wore a long blue dress with sleeve clasps. Clasps. As the word came into her head her hand felt under her pillow, but the clasp – was that what it was? – wasn't there. Panic. Then she saw it on the floor beside the bed. Picked it up, cradled it in her hand. Peace weave! Word weave! What was all that about? But the dream had gone again.

Dressing quickly, she put the clasp in one of the zipped pockets of her combats and hurried downstairs to the kitchen where Frank was making coffee. Fair Trade. He noticed her noticing the packet and shrugged.

"Try to do my bit."

Nanoushka, his cat, was rubbing round his legs. She wondered if the cat had been around when they all lived together.

"What are you doing today, honey?"

"Going to the dig."

"In this?" He nodded towards the window where rain was battering the glass. "And I'm not sure they work Sundays."

"I'll go and see." All the better if there was no one else there. She'd put back the brooch and leave.

Soon after breakfast, she found a waterproof among her things and headed off.

"Take this, honey." Frank handed her a key as she was about to close the door. "Tom and I might go out.

And mind how you go. There'll be a lot of folks hurrying to chapel this morning."

He was right about that. Cars slished past on the wet roads. Half the base seemed to be on the move. The other half were filling up at the motor pool – there was a bit of a traffic jam on the road – but the dig-site next door seemed empty.

Hopefully Hilde headed for Trench 3, behind the office, but there was someone there in day-glo water-proofs. It was Beth peering into the trench, and she looked up before Hilde could backtrack.

"Hello. You're keen! Come and look at this!"

What? The owner of the brooch? Hilde thought the heavy rain might have revealed a skeleton, but Beth was pointing at water in the bottom of the trench.

"It's on sand, so it'll drain away quickly, but while it's coming down there's not a lot we can do. Come on. Let's shelter for a bit and hope it stops."

No thanks, I think I'll be off home. Why couldn't she say that?

Instead she found herself following like a dog – to Beth's jeep parked behind some trees. Beth opened the passenger door for Hilde to climb in, and once they were both sitting in the cab, Hilde's lockjaw got worse. The clasp in her right-hand pocket was only inches from Beth's hand.

Beth was chatty.

"Don't suppose the others will turn up, not till this stops anyhow. Still, Meri's find yesterday was a good sign. If we find one body we usually find more, and at least we don't have to worry about so-called treasure seekers. Thieves,' she explained as Hilde felt her pulse rate accelerate. "They can be a big problem on digs. Usually, once we've opened a grave we have to rush to remove everything in one day, in case they turn up overnight and take what's left. But we can leave things in place here, and move them carefully, because security on base is so good. The military have put those up." She pointed to a couple of CCTV cameras one fixed to a tree, another on the side of a shed facing the trench.

Was it there yesterday? Was it switched on?

Beth drummed her fingers on the steering wheel, and Hilde felt herself go rigid as she said something about zero tolerance of theft. "A kid caught shoplifting for instance, can ruin a parent's career, so parents keep them in check. 'Scuse me." She reached into the glove compartment. and pulled out a piece of paper. "I thought you should have a copy of the form you signed yesterday. Bet you didn't read the small print. Have a read now." She handed it to Hilde and words jumped out. *All finds...must be handed immediately to the site supervisor*. She could feel Beth's eyes on her. Waited for a "Best hand it over".

The brooch felt hot beneath her fingers.

My good name is more precious than his gifts. Words from the dream were in her head. And words came to her lips. Beth, I forgot to tell you about this. But they wouldn't come out. The rain drummed on the roof of

46

the jeep. Oh I forget to mention this yesterday. But they stayed inside. If only she could say something, anything. The silence was embarrassing and Beth obviously felt it too because she suddenly switched on the engine making the windscreen wipers swish furiously. "I don't think this is going to stop, do you? We're going to have to call it a day. Can I drop you anywhere?"

"Washington Street. 281B." She managed that as jets filled the sky with thunder and black smoke.

Word weave. Peace weave.

But how could anyone peace weave here?

Beth swung the jeep towards the road. Five minutes later she dropped her at Frank's. "See you tomorrow with luck!" she shouted as she watched Hilde let herself in. "And say hi to Frank, will you, and tell him I'll be calling in for those books he ordered for me?"

But Frank wasn't in. Nor was Tom. Good. The house was blissfully quiet and empty. She could try and contact Ruthie in private. First she phoned, but there was no answer. Then she tried email, after setting up an account on Frank's computer. He'd said she could. He was falling over himself to please her, and hadn't mentioned school today.

Dear Ruthie,

Please get in touch. I need my shrink! I've done something stupid, probably because I'm going mad here and there is absolutely no one I can talk to. It's even worse than I thought, like being deported to a foreign country. I still can't believe Maeve has sent us to live here – though have to say Tom loves it – even though everyone's scared of terrorist attacks and planes are taking off for the Gulf all the time. It's obvious that the Americans are preparing for war. Mum has gone completely incommunicado. I haven't heard from her since I arrived. Please please please ask your mum to let me come and stay with you. I'll go mad if I stay here for much longer.

Love Hilde

P.S. Or come here. There's a guy you'd probably fancy. He's your type, tall as me, a bit like Tom in looks, sporty and he's got a fancy name, Friedman van Jennions.

She sent it to Ruthie's usual email address, hoping she had some means of accessing it in France. It wasn't a good letter, but having to be careful what she said about Maeve made her stilted. Maeve didn't want anyone else to know in case it got back to Tom and he worried. Before sending, she deleted 'go mad' and replaced it with 'have a nervous breakdown', which might get more response from Ruthie – if she got it. But, even if she did, it would be at least a fortnight before she could go and stay with her.

She spent the next few hours channel hopping and

playing mindless computer games – as the dream from last night flitted in and out of her head. Only one good thing – a phone call from Sylvie and Janey who said they couldn't make Wendy's tonight. She'd forgotten all about that. Neither Tom nor Frank came home at lunchtime. Frank had left a note saying they'd gone shopping. When they returned mid afternoon he gave her a present, gift wrapped.

"Hope it's what you want."

It was mobile, a pink one, small enough to fit in one of her zipped pockets, exactly what she would have chosen for herself.

"Thanks."

Tom said, "It's got Wap as well. So's mine, but don't worry about it costing. Frank says he's been putting money away for us. I was your personal shopper by the way."

He was already texting with his.

"It's perfect. Thanks." She gave him a hug.

"Frank bought it. Doesn't he get a hug?"

But Frank had made a diplomatic exit.

Later Tom and Frank went out to a movie. The male bonding was obviously going well. They invited her, but she said she had a headache. Her day had been a complete waste. She planned the next carefully, determined that nothing would stop her putting the brooch back. Before she got into bed, she checked it was safely in a zipped pocket in her combats, not under her pillow. She didn't want a repeat of the morning's 'where is it?' panic, or of the dream that had disturbed her day, but almost before her eyes had closed the voices were there.

"Y͟ou think my lord a milksop?"

The girl's blue dress glowed in the firelight.

"It is as I feared when I heard he had made the sleeve clasps," said the mother.

Mother and daughter wove words together while the messenger slept, and threads snapped from time to time. "And he did not defend your honour with his sword."

"He was keeping the peace at his father's bidding."

"And you want to break that peace by becoming a Shield Maiden?"

"What choice have I to defend my honour?"

"There may be other ways. Curb your wrath. Words are better than swords if we can find the right ones. Let us try to find them."

Now mother and daughter walked to the weaving house. There were stars above and a full moon, but the mother lit wall-torches for more light. Then, raising her eyes to the starry heavens, she called upon Wyrd, the Fate Weaver, to direct their fingers, and weave a fabric of peace. First they set up a loom with a warp of strong linen thread for the firmness of purpose they would need. Then they paused. By their side was a rack hung with skeins of wool all shades of the rainbow. Which would Wyrd choose?

As they waited for her to direct their fingers the moon appeared from behind a cloud. Where would her beams fall? As it lit up a bluebell blue — for the sea she must cross to reach her lord? For the dress she must wear when she met him? — Maethilde took it from the rack. And later as the moon travelled across the sky lighting up more colours one by one, she added red-gold, the colour of her hair, for herself crossing the sea. Then brown for a fort she must build when she reached the island shore — though the mother had some doubts about this. Then yellow-gold for the clasps he had given her, and more colours after that, for many fates crissed and crossed in that rich fabric. By dawn when they slept for a few hours, a tapestry half filled the loom but there were tangles in it.

"The stepmother is the knot that causes the tangles," mother and daughter agreed. "In the morning we must try to smoothe her."

"What is the stepmother's name?" the mother asked the messenger as she handed him bread and honey to break his fast.

"Eadith."

"Is she old like Manfried's father or young like me?" said Maethilde

"Older than you — she is grey-haired — but younger than he was."

"And is she a Peace Weaver?"

"She was when she married the father — and the son," said the messenger.

"And what does she like?" the girl asked.

"Like?" He looked puzzled.

"Does she like honey or jewels or copper pots?"

"She likes all of those things."

"And is there anything she likes more than those things?" said the girl. "I would like to take her a gift that would please her."

What he told her pleased her greatly. She sent for her brother Edwin and told him. Then she told the messenger she would return with him, and with her older brother and a hundred fighting men, for if she had to fight, she would. "But when we land you will go straight to Manfried and his stepmother. You will tell them I have come to take my place in the hall and bed of my lord as Peace Weaver."

Then mother and daughter went back to the weaving room. For three days and three nights Wyrd directed their hands to more shades of brown and grey than Maethilde herself would have chosen. And only Wyrd knew whether the dull hues — for the gift they would take to Eadith — would work their magic, but in the moonlight Maethilde's own colours, the blues and golds and reds she loved, seemed even brighter against the brown and greys. From time to time she touched her gold clasps — for the messenger had brought back the other — and they shone against the blue of the dress she wore as she wove the life of Manfried and Maethilde together. Peace weave. Word weave. She longed to begin.

Chapter 6

Peace weave, daughter. Word weave.

Hilde half woke, reluctant to let go of the colours in her head. The blue of the girl's dress was wondrous. She heard the girl's husky voice. Peace weave. But other voices began to compete. Gulf. Iraq. Tanks. Keeping her eyes closed, she tried to shut them out, glimpsed gold against blue. The sleeve clasps. The brooch! Eyes wide open, she remembered what she had to do, and scanned the room for her combats. They weren't on the back of the chair where she'd put them! Nor on the floor! Had she hung them in the cupboard? She flung open the door. No. Of course not. She hadn't put them there. She'd definitely put them on the back of the chair. So where were they? Under the bed? No. Someone had been into her room!

She flew downstairs. Frank was frying one of his specialities. French toast he called it. Tom was laughing. "Best call it Freedom toast now." He squeezed disgusting maple syrup over another slice.

"WHO took my combats out of my room?"

Tom raised a sticky finger. "You were asleep. They were muddy."

"Then where are they now?"

Tom shrugged.

"Honey, they're in the laundry."

"Laundry? The washing machine?"

Frank shook his head. "Sorry. Misunderstanding. They've gone to the laundry. Local firm fetches and delivers." There was a pile of clean clothes on a chair. "And I asked Tom to collect it up last night. So hands up, it's my fault."

"Surprise surprise."

He looked pained. Good.

"Laundry. Very liberated, Dad." Tom munched on.

"Haven't you got more pants, honey? What's the big deal?"

"My privacy! My property!" And something not my property, she didn't say, as she headed upstairs.

"They'll be back next Friday!" Frank called after her.

By which time she could have a criminal record. What would the brooch be like by Friday, she wondered. What would detergents and driers do to it? She had to get it back. How?

Word weave. Curb your wrath. Suddenly the dream

55

was in her head again. She took a deep breath. She must swallow her pride and talk to Frank. Hoping the right words would come, she headed downstairs again.

"There was something in the pocket," she explained to his back as he stacked the dishwasher. "A brooch. I've got to get it back. That's why I was so mad. Part of the reason anyway."

He straightened up and looked at her. "Why don't we talk about it?"

He turned down the sound on the TV.

"Later. When I've got my brooch back."

"I've sometimes left keys or coins in my pockets and they've always come back just fine, in a little plastic bag. What's this brooch made of?"

"Gold."

He raised a ginger eyebrow. "Who gave you that?"

She didn't answer and he didn't probe.

"Well, gold should be OK, and, honey, I've asked Tom not to go into your room without asking."

She said she'd like to ring the laundry, anyway, and he went to look for the telephone number. Luckily Tom, who might have asked more questions about a gold brooch, had already gone to play football with Friedman.

While she was ringing the laundry she heard the doorbell, and Frank opening the door.

"A "sort of" brooch you say?" The woman on the end of the phone had a local accent.

"Well I've made a note. Mr Browne's laundry will be

searched and anything found in the pockets will be packaged and returned to him."

"Can't I come and get it?" Now she could hear girls' voices in the hall. Oh no. Sylvie and co!

"It hasn't arrived at the depot yet, miss. The rounds man is still out, but you can be sure your brooch will be returned to you."

The line went dead as Frank walked into the diner followed by Sylvie and Janey and another girl with dark hair as short as a boy's.

"Trina," she said, sticking out her hand. "Pleased to meet you."

"Hilde."

All three girls were wearing green and white soccer strips.

"The Clickers," said Sylvie – or was it Janey? – tossing her ponytail and all three went into a routine. "Click beetles? Green and noisy – boom boom!" They laughed when Hilde didn't. "Now I know you said you weren't sporty, Hild." One of the twins flung her arm round her shoulders. "But we're desperate and figured you'd know the rules of soccer at least."

"Why?"

"Because you're British."

"And we think you'll look great in these," said Trina.

The three of them held up shirt and shorts like washing on a line.

"Excuse me, girls." Frank headed for the hallway. "Help yourselves to Cokes and cookies. I'm off to work."

"Ain't he cute?" said Trina as the door banged shut. Cute!

"You can ask him anything," she burbled, "anything, and he'll find the answer. Sometimes, when we were little kids..." – giggle stupid giggle – "we asked him, you know, silly questions, but he'd just hand over some book. "If all else fails, girls, use the index."" Her imitation of Frank's deep voice was crap.

"We're sorry about last night, by the way." One of the twins – Janey? – helped herself to a cookie from a jar. "We'd forgotten we had choir. Do you sing?"

Hilde shook her head, then froze as she caught sight of something on the still-silent TV screen. Maeve on the Human Shield bus. Part of her wanted to turn up the sound, but the picture changed before she could. It was definitely Maeve, though, on the bus. Other Stop the War campaigners were standing in front of it.

"Well, are you coming for a game? Have you got cleats?"

"Cleats?"

"Trainers," translated Sylvie. "You can change here or at the field. We're going straight there. School's closed because they're installing a new security system."

"9/11..." Trina began.

"I know," said Hilde. But why not go with them? There was no point going to the dig now, not without the brooch and a game of soccer might stop her feeling sick with worry. So Maeve and her fellow campaigners were on their way to Baghdad. They really thought they could stop the Americans bombing Baghdad, but could they? As if in answer a contingent of jets roared overhead. It was scary – she needed something to take her mind off that. Not that she wasn't proud. She wanted to yell, "That's my mum trying to stop this stupid war!" Instead she hurried upstairs to change her shoes.

The soccer ground was next to the football field. Friedman saw Hilde and the other girls arrive, though he should have been concentrating on coaching the Junior High kids. Hilde's bush of red-gold hair made her look a head taller than Trina Toner, who had the hots for him. She stopped and clung to the chain link fencing between the two grounds.

"Oooooh! Ooooh! There's the gorgeous Friedman!"

Silly Moo – he fancies me not you. Hilde was surprised at the thought in her head – and the smirk on her lips.

Friedman tried to focus on Tom's game, but saw Sylvie and Janey out of the corner of his eyes, dragging Trina away – and he saw Hilde striding after them in shorts!

"Good block, Tom!"

But Sylvie's voice carried on the wind. "He's got his mind on higher things, Trin!"

Did they know?

"Faster, Tom! No pain without gain!" Harley Green called out what he, Friedman, should have called out.

"Good pass, Tom!" Harley again – and the kid looked chuffed. He was a great kid and his sister was like a bear with a sore butt. Tom had told him about the row that morning.

"She'd have killed me if good old Frank hadn't stepped in."

Did he want to date a homicidal maniac?

"She went ballistic, because I picked up her filthy old combats and sent them to the laundry."

Did he want to date a girl who wore filthy pants?

He didn't. He did not!

Chapter 7

On Tuesday morning, Hilde woke up to the sound of Frank's raised voice – and it was Tom who was giving him hassle!

"I don't wanna get up. Why do I have to go to school if Hilde doesn't?"

"Because..."

She didn't hear the rest of Frank's reply, but Tom must have caved in because she heard him crashing about soon afterwards. She pretended to be asleep when he banged very loudly on her door. Later, the front door banged shut, and as the house went quiet, she thought they'd both gone out and it was safe to go downstairs, but Frank ambushed her in the kitchen. "Cappuccino, honey?"

He made good cappuccinos.

She nodded and he put it on the table. "Sit down, Hilde. We've gotta talk."

"What about?"

"School for starters."

She sat down and blew on the froth.

"I've checked out the pledge of allegiance. That was your objection, wasn't it? Well, you'll be pleased to know, they don't do it in High School."

"I'm still not going."

"May I ask why?" Saint Frank was super polite or sarcastic. She wasn't sure which.

"Because I'm not staying here. As soon as my friend Ruthie's back from skiing I'm going to stay with her."

"Who says? Your mom? Ruthie's mom? Have I been asked?"

"Why should you be?"

"I thought you and your mom were peace campaigners."

"We are."

"Well, I sure wish you did some of it at home!" And with that he left.

She spent the rest of the day trying to read some new books he'd brought her from the library, but his words kept intruding. *I thought you and your mom were peace campaigners.* They alternated with words from her dreams. *Peace weave. Word weave.* Well, she wasn't doing much of that. She wasn't gathering info for Maeve's Quaker friends. She wasn't trying to persuade people here that war was wrong. All she was doing was getting up people's noses. How useful was that? And later that evening she realised she might be scuppering her chances of returning the brooch to the site.

She was in the check-out queue at the 8 to 11 when she saw Beth and Sid. Or rather they saw her, when they came up behind her in the queue.

Sid, all smiles, said, "'Ello, 'ilde. You should come and see what we've found in your trench."

Beth, less smiley, said, "Don't, Sid. It looks as if Hilde's decided archaeology isn't for her."

"But it is!"

The quickness of her response took them – and her – by surprise. Sid laughed. It was as if her mouth was ahead of her brain. Or maybe it was the other way round. Anyway she suddenly realised that it would seem odd if she turned up Friday, after more than a week away without explanation and – there was something else. What had they found in her trench? She wanted to know.

"I'll come tomorrow, OK?"

As soon as she arrived she saw that the site was busier. There were more people. As Sid walked her over to 'her' trench, which he now called Trench 3, he said several new trenches had been opened up, by a group of archaeology students on work experience. Even from a distance, it was obvious that Trench 3 was much bigger now, a large square in fact. Sid didn't say what she was going to see, deliberately she couldn't help thinking, building up the suspense.

"Well?" They were there at last. He stuck out an arm dramatically. "There she is. Shield Maiden or Peace Weaver that be the question according to Meri."

Peace Weaver. A wisp of blue floated into her head as she looked onto a long, a very long skeleton which filled the far side of the square. Brown bones stood out against the chalky white soil.

"Well, 'ilde, what do you make of that?"

She was speechless. Nothing new there then.

"Ain't she bewdiful?"

Was this the owner of the brooch? Was this Maethilde, the girl in her dreams?

"We're almost certain it's female." Beth's words cut into her thoughts. She was standing on the far side of the trench, and seemed to be lecturing the students clustered round her. Then she saw Hilde and beckoned her over, pausing while she waited for her to join them. "As I was saying, we're almost sure it's female, despite its being so tall and with artefacts more associated with males."

She is female.

Looked at from directly above the skeleton didn't look quite so long, but the teeth and eye sockets in the domed skull looked even bigger.

"OK? Everyone listening?" Beth began lecturing again. "Now, we must never jump to conclusions about sex, height or anything else. Skeletons always seem very long at first sight because the feet are pointed down instead of out as they are in life. Some people thought this one was a giant! And I have to say she does seem taller than average. But she, if she was a she, was probably an Engle from Northern Europe. That's where the original English came from and they were a very tall tribe."

"What makes you think it's female?" a hairy male student asked.

"The tilt and width of the pelvis. You get a feel for these things after a while. And we can check our hunches. There's something called the sciatic notch on the other side of the pelvis, U-shaped in males V in women. And there's her jewellery, of course. See the cruciform brooches on her collarbones? Their position suggests that they pinned an outer to an inner dress or kirtle – and men didn't wear dresses. We'll have to move them very carefully. If there are threads attached we can discover the type and colour of the fabrics. See the beads too?" Beth pointed to a line of lumps between the two cruciform shoulder brooches.

Blue. Her dress is blue. It was her favourite colour. She didn't know about the beads.

"Men sometimes wore heavy brooches to pin cloaks, but they didn't generally wear necklaces. I think this was a very colourful lady. Move over, Claude. Let Sid get a close-up of those." Sid had been taking photographs for most of the time that Beth was speaking. "Note that we take photos of every stage of the dig. It helps with the record keeping."

Hilde wished he could photograph what she'd seen in her dreams, a woman with red-gold hair and pale freckled skin, wearing a dress of deep blue with sleeves of a lighter blue. Red and blue braid edged the hem and cuffs, and gold clasps linked the sleeve seams at the wrist.

"Look." Beth pointed to what looked like a rusty doorknob between two of the skeleton's ribs. "That makes me wonder if she really is female. It looks like a shield boss, but we don't come across many women buried with shields. And that," – she pointed to something else lying by the skeleton – "looks like a sword."

"It is possible that she was a warrior," said Meri, the blonde Norwegian archaeologist. "They called such women Shield Maidens."

Beth touched Hilde's arm. "You nearly discovered this yourself you know. Sid found it straightaway when we got back to work after the rain."

I did discover it.

"It's odd really, she's probably your height."

It's not just height we have in common.

Beth turned back to the others. "The only way to solve these questions – male or female, Shield Maiden or Peace Weaver is to get all this out, clean it up and get some lab evidence. But there's one find that doesn't need much cleaning. Has anyone spotted it? Look at her right wrist."

Hilde saw it straightaway.

"Is that gold?" said someone pointing to the other part of the clasp.

"Yes, and I think it's a very high quality sleeve clasp," said Beth, "for holding sleeve edges together. Very fashionable in the mid sixth century, so that helps us date the skeleton. And only women wore them, so that's a bit more evidence for the woman theory. So far we've only found one and they were usually worn in pairs. Perhaps we'll find the other when we dig a bit deeper under the left arm.

"As you'll see," Beth went on, "there are two linked square pieces and they worked a bit like cufflinks. They hold the sleeve edges together."

No, three linked pieces and the third bit, the brooch bit, is triangular.

"I've had a close look at this one," Beth went on, "and it's beautiful, an intricate arrangement of curves and spirals, which may be a stylised picture, carrying a message from the giver. Remember this was a pre-literate society except for some rune carving. People wouldn't have sent letters so their gifts were often messages. We mustn't ignore the possible symbolic value of any artefact, though we must also be careful not to project our own assumptions on to them."

"A deer for my dear.
My hart for your heart."

She heard the husky voice of her dreams. So that was it. The brooch did carry a message. Now words and images were flitting in and out of her head making it hard to concentrate on what was going on round her. Peace weave. Word weave.

Oh no, everyone was looking at her! She felt as if they could see the brooch through the window in her forehead.

"Would you mind, Hilde?" Beth smiled. "You were aeons away, weren't you? Meri suggested that you lie down beside the grave, so we can visualise how tall our skeleton was."

"Oh that's amazing," said Meri as Hilde lay down with her face on the earth. "Hilde looks as if she's worshipping Nerthus, as the woman in the grave probably did."

"Nerthus?" said a student.

"The Earth Mother," said Meri. "Do not tell me you have not heard of her. She was the Anglo-Saxons' most important deity."

Now an argument passed to and fro over Hilde's body.

"But weren't Tuw, Woden, Thor and so on, their main gods?"

Hilde remembered learning the same thing at school. The days of the week were named after them.

"No. They were minor gods," insisted Meri. "They each had a day of the week named after them. The Earth itself was named after Nerthus. The Anglo-Saxons were goddess worshippers. You must not forget this."

A girl student started to measure Hilde with a metre rod.

"And don't forget Frig," Meri went on, and several

students laughed. "She was also called Freya and was the goddess of love and fertility who gave us Friday. Some scholars think she and Nerthus became one over the years, which is why we have forgotten poor Nerthus."

"They're both 182 centimetres, Dr Stansfield."

"Beth, please."

"Wow! 6 foot 1," said someone else, staring at Hilde as she got up and brushed herself down, feeling like a freak.

Then Beth said, "Right, back to work, everyone! Let's leave Meri to get on. I want to know where that other sleeve clasp is."

I haven't got it! Hilde almost cried out. I didn't pinch that!

Guilt and a turmoil of other emotions made it hard to keep a grasp on reality. But Beth was right. There had been two clasps. She had seen them in her dreams, one on each of the young woman's sleeves. Suddenly another worry hit her. If they did find the other one, all three pieces, then they'd know there ought to be three bits to each clasp. They'd wonder where the third bit had gone. She hoped fervently they wouldn't find the other one before Friday, when with a bit of luck she'd get the brooch back from the laundry and return it to its owner in Trench 3.

That night, when she went to bed she yearned for sleep and a rest from her thoughts, but as soon as her head touched the pillow, blue, the colour of the summer sky, was in her head.

Maethilde was stitching the clasps to the blue dress, gold against blue like the sun in the summer sky, and as she sewed she called on Wyrd to weave summer into her life. Later she wrapped the dress in a linen sheet, laid it in her bride-chest and closed the lid. Then she called for bearers to carry the chest to the shore and she strode after them, her long legs bare and unhampered, for she wore a Shield Maiden's short tunic. She had said her goodbyes earlier. All the settlement had gathered to wish her god speed. Both Mother and Father had wished her farewell and her mother had urged, "Peace weave, daughter, if you can! Word weave!"

Now her words seemed to carry on the wind and merge with the sound of the sea.

"Peace weave! Word weave!"

"I will if I can, but what if he will not talk to me?" she had asked.

"If he sees you he will want to talk to you," her father replied.

"If you choose your words carefully he will listen," said her mother.

Now Maethilde could see her craft, Sea Wolf, afloat on the choppy waves, just off shore. So were two more small ships, for she had a hundred men in all, some already aboard the ships, others waiting on shore for her, among them her brother Edwin, two young dogs at his heels. All three ran forward as she approached. Edwin took her chest from the bearers and handed it to a youth, who carried it chest high to the ship. Now Sea Wolf looked eager to be off, and so did Maethilde. It was midsummer's night — the omens were good — and the heaving water glimmered silver and white. There was no time to waste. The moon was full and the tide was on the turn.

"To the ships!" She waded into the water and eager hands helped her aboard. Soon she stood at the prow, wind whipping her tied-back hair. Oarsmen sat ready.

"Pull!"

In minutes they were heading for the open sea, Sea Wolf leading the way.

"Hoist the sails!"

Maethilde had planned the campaign from start to finish and now she guided the fleet out into the North Sea. Reading the stars, she headed for the island where her destiny lay — to live or die Wyrd only knew. And Wyrd who wove the fates of everyone, wove the winds, which billowed the red sails and shot them swiftly through the water. Too swiftly some said. They surged through the floodways, tossing on the terrible waves, but after three days and nights they had seen no land, and some began to think they had passed the island in the dark. There were mutterings in the ranks as seabirds screeched overhead. What did Maethilde know about seafaring? She had never sailed far from the mouth of the Elbe before.

And then on the morning of the fourth day, as the sea-mists thinned, a curved coastline took shape before them, a black bulge of land changed to green as they got closer to the woods covering it. Hand on helm, Maethilde guided the vessel round the coast to the mouth of a river. Then, mindful of her troops' safety, she bade the men land and build a fort close to the river's edge, yet not so far from the sea that they could not make a quick escape if need be. And they built in haste, with wood brought with them ready cut, for Maethilde had thought hard about this too. Fired by honour and friendship for her lord, her heart ruled, but her head stayed cool. From the messenger she'd learned that Manfried and the stepmother lived inland, a day's walk away along the riverbank. But she waited till her men were safely inside the fort, their ships hidden ready for escape if need be, before sending the messenger to his and her lord.

"Tell my lord Manfried that the lady Maethilde has come to take her place as his wife-man. Tell him that his betrothed has come in peace, and wishes to talk — with him and with his stepmother if she wishes, and that I bring gifts for them both as proof of my goodwill. Tell him I come as Peace Weaver, but in all fairness tell him also that I am armed and ready to fight for what is my right. It is his choice to meet me as Peace Weaver or Shield Maiden, to take his place in my arms or at the end of my sword."

It was three days before the messenger returned. As she waited Maethilde's hopes fell. Fearing the worst she sharpened her sword and drilled her troops on the shore. On the third day, looking out from the ramparts, she saw the messenger running towards the gates of the fort. As he staggered in, pointing behind him, she knew her worst fears were realised. For a forest of spears was emerging from the woods.

"They ... my lord and ... say the lady Maethilde must leave now," gasped the messenger. "You are out-numbered! Manfried has an army three hundred strong of Engles and Mercians both, for the stepmother sent for reinforcements from her own tribe. If you value your own life, I beg you, get in your boats and leave!" he cried, but Maethilde had picked up her sword.

Seabirds screamed as she ordered her men to take up arms.

Chapter 8

The screech of aircraft shattered Hilde's angry dream. Windowpanes rattled as she glanced at her bedside clock. The date caught her eye first. Friday.

"FRIDAY!"

She was out of bed and on the stairs before the doorbell rang, but Frank got to the door first. The laundryman was handing over a pile of clothes in plastic bags.

"It's OK, honey, here's what you've been waiting for." Frank handed her a small packet. "And here are your pants. I bet you've never seen them look that good."

She raced upstairs, dumped the combats on the bed, tore open the packet and nearly cried with relief. Perfect. It seemed like a miracle.

A deer for my dear!

My hart for yours!

All – all! – she had to do now was put it back.
Anywhere.

As she hurried to the site jets screamed overhead and the
air stank of kerosene. A grey haze masked a wintry sun,
but – she urged herself to think on the bright side – at
least it wasn't raining. As she walked she wondered
where she'd be working. Trench 3 was too much to hope
for. The experts seemed to have taken that over. For the
last two afternoons she'd been working in Trench 6,
with a girl called Libby, who was a heavy smoker. As the
site came into view she thought of a plan. Libby often
went off for a smoke, which wasn't allowed on the site,
and it would be easy to push the brooch into her side of
the trench during one of her absences, making sure she
wasn't in the sights of the CCTV of course. When Libby
found it she'd be ecstatic.

But Beth scuppered that plan as soon as she arrived in
the office.

"Would you mind helping with a new trench, Hilde?
Near the finds shed. Finish signing in and I'll take you
over. Sid's been showing a new volunteer what to do but
we need him to lift something fragile in Trench 3."

Hilde collected her tools and followed.

"I thought you could keep an eye on the new guy. As
a general policy we don't put girls and guys in the same
trench but…"

Hilde's eye was already on him.

"Just make sure he takes his time," Beth went on.

74

"Guys tend to think it's a race."

They arrived at the new trench. He was on his knees.

"Friedman, meet Hilde. She's one of our regulars."

Friedman. Manfried.

Hilde. Maethilde.

Why hadn't she noticed that before?

"We know each other thanks. Hi, Hilde."

He smiled up at her.

"Oh good," said Beth, setting off back to Trench 3. "You're OK for a bit then?"

She called over her shoulder, "Any problems, Friedman, ask Hilde. She knows what to do."

Know what to do? Hilde hadn't a clue what to do. She was fighting feelings she'd never had before. He was gorgeous with eyes like dark chocolate and long, long lashes.

No, NO. He wasn't. Perv – he was staring at her legs.

He wasn't, well only for a second, before moving swiftly to her face via her shirt, a less hostile one today he thought but couldn't be sure – because the sun suddenly broke through the grey, making a silhouette of her figure! Working together! In the same trench! What amazing luck. His plan had more than paid off already. Yesterday he'd found out from Tom that this was where she spent most of her time. Today he'd skipped study hall because he had to see her again. Had to – to make a rational judgement about her, because he couldn't get her out of his mind. Day or night. He kept seeing her in his dreams where every inch of her was stunning. Every inch. So, one, check her looks. Two, check her personality, because even if she was stunning that wasn't enough. Personality was important too. Looks can deceive.

"Excuse me." She dropped into the trench – like a lioness!

"Have you got a tool?" She wished she hadn't said that.

He wished she hadn't said that. "H-here." He handed her a trowel, picked up something else and started to scrape soil.

Hilde's face burned. Why had she said something so crass? Why was her hand shaking? Concentrate. But it was hard concentrating when the coincidence of their names was still jumping around in her head – what did it mean? – and another bum was inches from her own. And not any old bum, but his bum. Libby's hadn't mattered. Libby! She remembered her plan. It could still work. Even better to let Fried Man find the brooch! But she needed him out of the way while she buried it near where he was working.

"Do you smoke?"

"No." He turned, surprised. "Do you?" he asked her back.

"No."

Friedman wanted to capitalise on his initial good luck. But conversation wasn't exactly flowing. Or even trickling. Concentrate on your plan. One, check looks. Well he would if she'd turn round. Two, check personality. He didn't want to carry on with this digging without good reason. He hated the dirt under his fingernails. He'd got a a blister in the palm of his hand. Wasn't digging holes a form of penal servitude in some states? Penal servitude. He remembered a Hershey's bar in his pocket.

"D'ya like chocolate, Hilde?" Turn round, please.

"Yes." Perhaps he'd go and buy some?

"Here then." He touched her elbow, and she jumped as if stung. But she did turn round and he was drowning drowning in her gorgeous, gorgeous bluebell eyes.

He was staring at her face which was turning into a red blob. She could feel her freckles flowing into each other, and she could see herself in his pupils, so big and black. Two little Hildes. Why was he staring? Why was she staring back? Why couldn't she move? Why was her heart thumping?

Hilde and Friedman. They went well together.

No they don't.

"Chocolate?"

She noticed the bar in his hand.

"Thanks," she mumbled when her mouth was empty, though she hadn't meant to accept it, and most of it was stuck in her throat. But at least eating broke the spell. The spell? Was that what it was, the feeling she was in his power? Dark hair, brown eyes. Don't look at his eyes. He wasn't even her type. He was Ruthie's type. She looked at his trainers. Nike.

"Aren't they full of CFCs?"

"No, they changed the formula." Friedman didn't mind that she was on the attack again. At least there was some connection, and now he had to keep it going.

"What's so great about archaeology then? Can't see the attraction myself." He held out his hands in a spoof of a prissy girl. "It's ruining my hands!"

Wrong tack. She didn't laugh, and his voice had gone dangerously off key. Deep breath. Try again. "It looks OK on TV I guess, when they keep finding valuable stuff."

"'snot about cash!"

"I didn't mean..."

"You're so materialistic!"

For chrissake! Temper like a cut snake. So mission accomplished. He'd checked. She had a rotten personality. She was stuck up, humourless and bad tempered, and her face was like a lobster, boiled. Good, now he could get out of the trench, make his excuses to Beth and Sid and never come back!

"Goodbye. I hope archaeology brings you intense spiritual satisfaction."

"Good riddance!" She carried on working, aware of him striding away.

Hilde and Friedman.

Friedman and Hilde. They went well together. No they do not!

Chapter 9

Sid came over soon after Friedman had left the site, but didn't comment on his absence. Probably thought he'd gone to the loo. He was excited about something.

"Come and see what we've found now, 'ilde. Meri thinks it might be a bed."

He led her back to Trench 3 which was much bigger than when Hilde had last seen it. The skeleton filled less than half of it now. Beth was on her knees near its head, measuring something. She seemed even more excited than Sid.

"The bit we think is a bedhead is already more than a metre long. So it might even be a double bed with someone else in it." She wrote something on her squared pad and climbed out. "Hilde, I thought you'd be a good person to help Meri."

79

"Hello, Hilde." Meri stood in the shallow, newly-opened part of the trench, watching someone else working near the skeleton's shoulder.

"That's Amy," Beth said. "She's the new finds supervisor."

"Hi, Hilde." The other person didn't look up. All Hilde could see of her was a mousy ponytail and a tartan shirt.

"Amy's started cataloguing all the artefacts we've found," Beth went on, "though right now she's doing a bit of hands on. As you can see most artefacts have gone from this grave. The sword's gone to the lab for cleaning. We think there's something odd about it. It isn't pointed and Amy thinks it may have been made into a weaving batten. Swords into weaving battens! Don't you like the sound of that?"

"Yes," said Hilde and meant it. "I do."

Meri explained what she wanted Hilde to do. "As you can see the machine has taken off the topsoil from the newly opened bit. Now we must move the rest very carefully." She pointed to a row of rusty metal lumps running parallel with the skeleton's left side. "They're what first alerted me. I think they're the remains of iron plates used to hold two pieces of a wooden frame together. With luck a few fragments of wood might still be attached. Most will have rotted away, but note how the colour of the soil is different there."

Hilde pointed to a darker seam at right angles to it. "Is that what Beth thinks is the bedhead?"

"Yes. Well done. Beth said you had a good eye. Try not to disturb it and keep a lookout for more metal fittings. The aim is to expose them at this stage, not remove them. There might be textile attached to some of the metal, indicating that it was upholstered. Quite a comfortable bed in fact."

Hilde worked at the top end of the bed, if it was a bed, next to the skeleton's head. If there was someone else in it he was just beneath her. Manfried. Was that his name?

Manfried and Maethilde.

Friedman and Hilde.

She couldn't get the names out of her head. Maethilde lay in arm's reach on her right. She could have put back the brooch if Amy and Meri hadn't been there. Soon Amy started talking to Meri – as if Hilde weren't there fortunately.

"Beth said you had a theory about Shield Maidens – was it – and Peace Weavers?"

"Yes, the two types of women keep popping up in the old Germanic stories. The Shield Maiden, she is the fierce virgin, often fighting by the side of the men, but otherwise keeping them at spear's length. The Peace Weaver was usually married, because, in fact, marriage was an act, many acts of peace weaving, bringing families and sometimes warring tribes together. Women had to weave words very skilfully to keep the peace. They were the diplomats who, you could say, wove the fabric of society."

Hilde listened hard.

"What's this lady, then?" Amy nodded towards the skeleton. "Peace Weaver or a Shield Maiden?"

"I am not sure. When I saw the shield and sword I thought, Shield Maiden, but now that you say the sword may have been a weaving batten…"

As Hilde listened she willed Meri and Amy to go away, if only for a minute, so she could put the brooch back, and Meri did get out of the trench once, but only to have a good stretch and then go and crouch beside Amy. "You know Wagner's Ring Cycle? Well, Brunnhilde was a Shield Maiden. She put a ring of fire round herself to keep men at bay. Oh, Hilde…" She smiled down at her. "Brown Hilde. Hilde Browne. What a funny coincidence."

Funny? Coincidence? The Ring Cycle was one of Frank's favourite CDs. She sometimes wondered what the woman on the cover was doing. She looked as if she was burning alive.

By the end of the day the experienced archaeologists were almost certain they'd found a double bed, a very rare find.

"But no second body yet?" Beth asked when she came to add to her records.

"He's probably under your feet, 'ilde," said Sid, arriving with a metal detector. "We'll have a look tomorrow, but first let's try this."

As Meri and Amy got out of the trench he stepped in.

"Not a beep," he said after going over the surface

twice. "If there's anyone there they're not buried with weapons. Nor are they wearing any metal jewellery, which is odd considering all the stuff buried with the lady."

"But why was she buried on a double bed if there isn't anyone else?" said Beth.

"Hoping to meet someone nice in the next world?" said Amy.

Sid shrugged. "Who knows? Come on. I'm ready for something to eat."

He passed the metal detector up to Beth and as it moved close to Hilde it started to whine. He laughed. "What you hiding, 'ilde?"

She felt her face burning as everyone stared at her. There was quite a crowd round the trench now. As people left off work they stopped off at Trench 3 to see the star find.

Beth's voice broke the silence.

"Before you go, everyone, we've got a few places in the minibus for the trip to West Stow tomorrow. It's a reconstructed Anglo-Saxon village, built on the site of a settlement discovered a few years back, and they're having an Open Day. You'll see how the people we're digging up dressed, what their houses were like, what they ate and so on. Anyone like to come?"

Beth's voice seemed a long way off. No one said, 'Empty your pockets, Hilde.' But she felt as if Sid had seen the brooch, as if it was an X-ray machine in his hand, not a metal detector.

Chapter 10

Frank was in the kitchen when she got back, wearing a striped apron.

"Crab chowder, have you had that before?" He consulted the recipe propped in front of him. "Oh, and there's a letter for you with a German stamp."

It was on the table. She grabbed it.

"Got a pen-pal, have you?"

"Sort of." Racing upstairs, she tore it open cursing the fact that post wasn't delivered on base. There was no privacy here. Frank collected it each day from the Post Office, so there was no chance of getting it before he did. But it was from her mum! The block capitals and flowery pink stationery were part of her cunning disguise. The postcard inside with a Scottish scene on it – for Tom – was another. She took it straight to him.

Back in her room she read eagerly.

Dearest Hilde,

How are you? What are you doing with yourself? I'm fine. The spirit on board the bus is wonderful and we get lots of support as we travel through Europe. I'm sorry I haven't rung you but it's difficult from here and I can't believe that the phones aren't all tapped where you are. I just hope private correspondence is safe. I do understand how difficult it is for you – my idea of hell in fact – but hope you've forgiven me for not letting you come with me. I'm sure you have. You've always been so supportive of my peace work, and seemed to understand, even as a little girl, that this is something I have to do.

The words blurred. Blow nose. Grit teeth. Carry on.

And, darling, as I said, you can be useful on base. I don't expect you've won any hearts and minds for the cause – perhaps best not to try in the circumstances, not on the base, but maybe off it? Do you get off it? Anyway, I do hope you've managed to gather some info about security on base? Myra Jenkins and co would love to get on to Whiston Base, to protest against the increasingly belligerent stance of the USA – and our own government – who seem hellbent on war with Iraq. A demo ON base would also prove to the authorities how easily a group of terrorists could break in and gain access to nuclear bombs. Have you observed, for instance, how frequently the perimeter fence is patrolled? Are there regular times for this or do they do random checks? If random, how long is the minimum time between patrols? With info like that, campaigners could estimate how long they'd got to cut through the wire, before the military arrive. They would expect to get caught of course – they'd <u>intend</u> to get caught – but not before they were inside with access to weapons. It would be excellent publicity for the Stop the War campaign, which is even more important now. War with Iraq would kill innocent civilians and incite terrorists. It would increase the number of attacks, make 9/11s more likely not less. Do you think you could send this info to the address enclosed?

No! I can't!

You can send letters to me to the same address. Friends will forward them.
Peace and lots of love,

Mum

But I haven't got that sort of info. Can't get it. Maeve hadn't a clue, though she ought to have. Didn't she know Frank's house was in the middle of the base? You couldn't see the perimeter fence even from an upstairs window. Sick with guilt, the knot in her stomach tightened. She hadn't won any hearts and minds either. Hadn't tried. Maybe she ought to start going to school and start talking to other kids? She'd heard Tom saying some kids were seeing counsellors, they were so worried about their dads and mums getting killed. Maybe they'd be prepared to think about other ways of solving disputes. Scared of their parents dying? She knew how they felt.

But what was the point of trying to persuade kids on base that war was wrong? How could they stop the war? How could anyone stop it? As she reached for a tissue to blow her nose, her hand brushed the brooch and a flash of her dream was in her head. Maethilde with sword held high, watching an army of three hundred men coming out of the woods. Was the urge to fight unstoppable, even when you wanted to be a Peace Weaver?

She spent the evening trying to write a letter to Maeve, explaining why she couldn't help, but eventually gave up, got ready for bed and pulled the duvet over her head – and there was Maethilde again.

As she watched from the ramparts of the fort, the timber beneath her hands felt hot and dry. Was there time to get her men to throw more water on the fort? More and more weapon-men were emerging from the forest. One of their flaming arrows could set the fort alight.

If her men stayed here they'd be burned alive. If they fought on the beach they'd be slaughtered.

A forest of spears was approaching, an army three times bigger than hers was racing towards them. She thought quickly. What if an archer let loose an arrow before her lord was close enough to hear her words of peace and friendship? What if he never discovered she came to weave peace?

Heading for the stairs, she made a sudden decision. "Tell the troops we will meet the enemy outside on the beach," she told her brother, "not get roasted within. And get bearers to bring me my chest. I will give peace weaving one last chance."

Soon her men were assembled on the beach. Behind them, well hidden, were the boats. She had ordered her troops to prepare for escape, theirs not hers, for she had told them all many times that she had come to the island to live or die with honour. Her good name, that is what she had come for.

"Three hundred against one hundred!" cried Edwin. "Let us leave straightway, and return later with more men."

But his sister would hear none of it.

"That would be a going back," she said — in every sense — to the days of raids and skirmishes. "I have come as a Peace Weaver to tie threads not break them."

And now she was dressed as a Peace Weaver, for she had put aside her leather fighting tunic and Shield Maiden's helmet, and had taken from her chest the dress of summer blue. Shield Maiden she might have to be, but she wanted Manfried's first sight of her to be as Peace Weaver, his wife-man in her long blue dress with the sleeve clasps he had made for her. Hurriedly she had piled her red-gold hair on the top of her head, and fixed it with the walrus tusk combs he had sent her. Now she took her place in front of her troops. The yellow sand stretched out in front of her. The sea on her left seemed to speak.

Peace weave. Peace weave.

Where was her lord? He must be the helmeted figure at the front of the approaching force. The Grey Hair beside him must be the stepmother. Nose and cheek guards masked his face, even his eyes, lost in shadow. Even when he halted his troops fifty paces from hers, she could not see his eyes though she looked straight at them.

He could see hers though, bluer, much bluer than the sea heaving at their side. As blue as the bluebells in the forest in springtime. The sight of her standing at the head of her troop of warriors stopped him in his tracks, though the stepmother was urging him forward. But Maethilde's red-gold hair was gleaming in the sunlight, tendrils curling and waving in the sea breeze. And like the sea, the blue of her dress was softly rising and falling.

His mouth felt dry. His pulses raced. He'd expected to see her brother at the fore, not her. And that must be her brother at her side, standing slightly back bearing sword and shield — and another sword and shield lay at his feet. Were they her weapons? The messenger had said she was prepared to fight for what was right, in single combat, for she didn't want others to lose their lives fighting for her rights. She was a doughty fighter, he'd said.

89

She had trained hard as Shield Maiden. But how could he fight her when he wanted to hold her in his arms?

His stepmother-wife hissed into his left ear.

"Put the girl and her raiders to rout. Drive them back to their ships. There are three hundred fighting men behind you, Engle and Mercian." Her tribe had sent troops too to back up her claim. "Mercia will not let this foreign upstart take my place."

Chapter 11

When Hilde woke up she knew she'd been dreaming, but the dream refused to reappear, though she kept her eyes tightly shut. TV and other morning sounds intruded. So did memories of the previous evening. The floor beside her bed was littered with crumpled attempts at writing letters and not just to Maeve.

Dear Tony Blair,

What if Cherie was in Baghdad right now? Would you still be going to war? What would <u>your</u> children think if you gave orders for bombs to be dropped on their mum? Well, my mum IS there, and so are thousands of Iraqi mums...

But if she sent it some aide would read it, not him.

"Honey!" Frank was knocking at her door. "Beth's here."

"Why?" Had she found out about the brooch!

"She seems to think you said you wanted to go on the trip to the Anglo-Saxon village!"

Hilde peered out of the window. The minibus was outside with Sid in the driver's seat.

"Well, I didn't."

"But why don't you, honey? There's a spare place. I might come too."

"No thanks. You go."

"But, honey..."

"My name's Hilde. HILDE! You should know!"

Pause.

"Sure. It's a beautiful name."

She heard him going downstairs.

Two miles away in Pyghtle Cottage Friedman was having an altercation with his mom.

"Friedman, I planned this outing for you!" Marty van Jennions raked her blonde hair. "Yesterday you were all fired up by archaeology."

"Sorry, Mom. You got the wrong idea. I was giving it a try, and I found it wasn't for me."

Too right it wasn't. He never wanted to see that bad-tempered giant again.

Marty appealed to her husband. "Karl, we're all going. We're having lunch there. Can't you persuade him?"

"Dad, I've got football. I promised I'd go."

And Dad – good old Dad – didn't pull rank for once. "I'm sure you're gonna miss something great, son, but…" He shrugged.

"We're going to eat Anglo-Saxon food and and… everything," said Olivia.

"Honey." Her father tugged one of her pigtails. "Leave it. Friedman doesn't want to come."

Hilde changed her mind. She wasn't sure why, but suddenly the prospect of a lonely day worrying seemed even less attractive than wandering about what she thought would be a museum. But it wasn't a museum. In fact, the re-constructed village was much more interesting than she'd anticipated. Did Maethilde live in a settlement like this, she wondered as she followed Frank, Beth and Sid from one thatched wooden building to another, stopping to watch a shoemaker or a blacksmith or a potter from time to time? The buildings were grouped in a rough circle round an expanse of grass where hens scratched and children played ball and hide-and-seek.

Did Maethilde eat food like they were eating, well like the others were eating, she wondered as she stood by the central fire, munching on a chunk of bread, not unlike modern granary bread? The others were eating mutton stew off wooden platters. A young woman dressed in Anglo-Saxon clothes had filled the platters from the pot hanging over the fire, rolling up her long sleeves to stop them hanging in the stew. With her long blonde hair in plaits, she looked as if she might have stepped out of the past. Now she explained that they were in the hall, which was a sort of sitting cum dining room.

Beth had already said, as they walked around, that all the buildings had separate functions, much as rooms in modern houses had separate functions. The hall was possibly the most comfortable building, she said, now pointing to the woven hangings on the walls and the cushions on the benches. But when they went next door, to the sleeping house, Hilde thought that looked even cosier.

"The whole family would have slept here," said the bearded old man, who sat in the doorway. "Children on the raised platform filling the left-hand side, the parents on the opposite side." He pointed to a double bed quite like a modern one – and Hilde saw a woman standing by it fingering the sleeve clasp on her blue dress, a tall woman, amazingly like the Maethilde of her dreams.

"Note how we've hung curtains from the beam in front of the bed," the old man went on, "to give the man and his wife a bit of privacy and keep out draughts, and just make the place look nice. The Anglo-Saxons liked their textiles and the wife would have woven them of course."

Man. Wife. Hilde looked to see if the man was around, but couldn't see the woman either now. Where had she gone? Hilde looked to see if there was another door at the back, but there wasn't. There was just the one at the front, and if the woman had left by that she'd have passed close by. They'd all have seen her. Hilde froze. What had she seen? Had anyone else seen it? She wanted to ask but the others were still listening to the old man who was talking about bed covers.

"What's on the bed behind you?" Beth asked, pointing to a silvery fur on a single bed in the corner.

"A wolfskin." He patted it. "That's my bed. Grandparents did live with the family, sometimes, but they were a bit of a rarity because life expectancy was only about thirty-five years. That's why people got married so young, at fourteen or fifteen. In those days grey hair was a source of wonder."

A source of wonder. Hilde wondered what she had seen as she followed the others out of the building. The woman had been like the Maethilde of her dreams, but she hadn't been sleeping. She'd been wide awake.

In a daze she followed the others outside, heard someone say it was raining. Heard Beth say, "Let's go to the cinema then, back in the reception building. We should probably have gone there first. There's a video worth watching, that gives an excellent introduction to the village."

As the lights dimmed Hilde was glad of the darkness. Rippling harp music washed over her as the screen glowed with the flames of a fire. "Have you ever wondered how the Anglo-Saxons lived?" said a voice-over, as the picture changed to a fire-lit hall, like the one where they'd eaten their lunch, but now it was full of people with brightly coloured clothes, their bronze brooches gleaming in the firelight. Then abruptly the music stopped and an aerial view of the village replaced the scene in hall. "When archaeologists excavated the original village of West Stow they found lots of evidence for a peaceful scene like the one you have just seen," the voice-over continued, "but no evidence for the battles, often mentioned in history books. The skeletons unearthed bore no signs of battle injuries. In fact all the evidence points to there having been a peaceful, co-operative community here, and we now think that Angles, Saxons, Frisians and Romano-Britons and maybe other tribes lived peacefully together here, side by side at first, then mixing and marrying. There seems, in short, to have been more peace weaving than pillaging."

Afterwards, Hilde couldn't remember leaving the cinema or walking to the weaving house, but she did remember seeing Frank bump into Lieutenant-Colonel Karl van Jennions on his way out. She'd just told Frank she wanted to stay and watch the weaving demonstration again, mostly because she wanted to be on her own to think about what she had seen in the sleeping house. Hoping Frank wouldn't mention that she was there, she hung back in the shadows. From the corner of her eye she saw the lieutenant-colonel come in with a woman and two little girls, who soon found their way to the front of the people watching.

"I'm going to start by making a length of braid," said the woman demonstrator. "Anglo-Saxon women liked edging their clothes with braid. I'm mixing dark and light green wool, both of which I've dyed with nettles."

"And do you use exactly the same dyes as the Anglo-Saxons used?" said a loud American voice. Hilde guessed whose.

"Definitely," the demonstrator replied. "The yellow is from gorse flowers, the blue from woad and the red from madder root."

Madder. The word made Hilde feel sick. Was she going mad? *You need one friend, Hilde, someone to talk to, or you'll go mad*. But she hadn't made any friends. And now she was seeing things. And hearing things. Voices. Maethilde's voice. Peace weave. It was the brooch. Her guilty conscience. She must put it back.

The demonstration ended. People spilled out. Hilde watched where most people were going and set off in the opposite direction. Finding herself back in the reception building, she saw a sign for a costume exhibition. It might be a good place to think. She needed to be quiet and on her own. Her mind was in turmoil. Words filled her head. And as she stepped inside she activated more words, a recorded commentary. She hurried past but the words kept on. "In sixth-century East Anglia women were wearing clothes and jewellery like those worn by the three models in front of you. Note the long under and overdresses, joined at the shoulder with brooches. Note the girdles round their waists, so the women could hitch up their skirts in muddy weather." Pursued by the voice, she moved further away, to the far end of the room to a glass cabinet, full of sleeve clasps. A caption beneath one pair said, "Fashionable in the mid sixth century. Square pieces held together the sleeve edges and the three-sided brooch was for ornament." It was like the one in her pocket but not as lovely.

"Bewdiful, ain't they?"

Hilde jumped. The voice behind her was American.

"It is Hilde? Hilde Browne, Frank's daughter?" A short-haired blonde woman with glasses beamed up at her. "Sorry to give you a fright. I'm Marty van Jennions. I thought I recognised you in the weaving house. I've just been speaking to Frank and I'm delighted to say, I've persuaded him to come back to our place for supper. The girls are just thrilled they're gonna meet you. And Tom's there already with Friedman."

No! The words were on her lips but wouldn't come out. No, no, no!

Chapter 12

So she followed like a zombie, got into the back of Marty's station wagon with Frank and the two little girls who snuggled up to her as if she were their big sister.

"Seat belts, girls, then we'll be homeward bound." Karl drove while Marty kept up a running commentary about the scenery. The journey was only a couple of miles. Hilde was dismayed when they arrived a few minutes later.

Pyghtle Cottage was quite like the buildings in Stow except that the wattle walls were plastered and painted white and the thatched roof had a chimney.

"Only sixteenth century!" Marty laughed as she showed them in through the kitchen door. "A whole thousand years later than the Anglo-Saxons." She asked her girls to take Frank and Hilde to the sitting room where they both had to duck to miss the low beams.

"The meal won't be long. Karl, will you call the boys, please?"

Cally soon joined her mother in the kitchen, but Olivia stayed close to Hilde.

"I like your hair." She flicked her own plaits as if trying to get rid of them. "I wish mine was curly. Let's sit in the inglenook." She led the way to seats either side of the fire, unlit, but laid with twigs and logs. "It's not fair. I help collect the wood, but I'm not allowed to light it. Only Friedman is."

Friedman. Man friend. Friend man. Fried man. Hilde the wordless was suddenly full of words, jumping around in a crazy game of anagrams. She remembered their last meeting. Goodbye. Good riddance.

Tom appeared. "Hi, Sis." He was holding some sort of computer game and looked really happy.

And then Friedman came into the room. Avoiding his eyes – not difficult because he was obviously avoiding hers – Hilde started talking hairstyles with Olivia.

He got matches and lit the fire, fed the leaping flames with twigs, kneeling inches from her knees. Olivia was talkative thank goodness. She changed the subject to fairies, fire fairies who she reckoned lived up the chimney. Then Marty came in and told them to take their places at table in the dining room, and somehow Hilde and Friedman were standing next to each other.

100

"Now if you'll all link hands…" Marty stood at one end, her husband at the other. "Karl will say grace."

They closed their eyes and Hilde felt Olivia's hot little hand grab hers. On her other side Friedman's fingers hardly touched, but sent shivers up her arm. As his father asked the Lord to make them truly thankful she sneaked a look – and found Friedman looking at her.

Grace over, Marty seemed to sense some awkwardness.

"The hand linking's my bit of peace weaving I suppose," she said, as if in explanation. "Don't you just love that concept? I think it makes for more peaceful meal times anyhow. Now, Hilde, what can I get you? It's Boston baked beans from the *Moosewood Cook Book*. Frank said you were a vegetarian. There's ham with it for the carnivores."

Hilde stammered a reply, and as Marty filled her plate she noticed, on the wall opposite above Frank's head, a cross-stitched "Blessed are the Peace Makers". Next to it were photographs of men in uniform, all vaguely familiar. It looked as if the van Jennions family had been in the US military for generations.

"Several of my mother's friends," Hilde found her voice at last, "in the Peace Movement – they do it – link hands – say grace – all that – but they – most of them are Friends, Quakers, they try to live – enact their Christian beliefs."

Tom glared at her from across the table.

Marty was a ladle-bearing statue.

Frank said, "Would you like to rephrase that, honey?"

Then Marty smiled. "I think I know what Hilde's getting at." She glanced at the cross-stitched quotation. "But maybe we're talking about two different things. The peace of Jesus Christ is surely different from political peace?"

"In what way?" Hilde was surprised to find the words still coming.

"What's the Peas Movement?" said Olivia.

Hilde listened as Lieutenant van Jennions said some people believed you should never take up arms even if another country invaded yours. "They believe that when someone hits your cheek, you should offer them the other one."

"Like it says in the Bible?" said Olivia.

"It's an active thing. Pacifism isn't p-a-ss-i-vism." Hilde spelled it out. "You do things to promote peace. And you protest peacefully like Gandhi. It isn't appeasement. It isn't giving in to bullies and dictators."

"Then how do you get rid of them?" said Frank. "That's the big question. As George Orwell said, pacifism just plays into the hands of dictators. Lie down in front of them Gandhi-like, and they stamp on your face – or get their henchmen to do it, and worse. Dictators haven't got consciences and you can't negotiate with them. They lie. Think of Hitler."

"But Saddam Hussein isn't Hitler. He hasn't invaded another country."

"He did in '90," said Karl.

"So…" She chose words carefully. "It was probably right to push him back into his own country, when he invaded Kuwait. War might be right sometimes, as a last resort. I'm for peace weaving, and that might not be the same as pacifism. I think it may be right to have armies for defence, but surely it's not right to be an aggressor? It wouldn't be right to invade Iraq now? Do you think it would be right?"

Silence.

Friedman waited for his dad to reply, fascinated.

"I serve my country, Hilde."

"Right or wrong?"

"I'm in the military. I do what my President asks."

"Right or wrong?" she insisted.

"I do my duty. I'm a patriot."

Friedman had heard the words before but never questioned them, but now it was as if someone – Hilde – had clicked a switch in his head. That answer wasn't good enough. Didn't his dad think about what he was doing? She had opened his eyes, his heart, his mind. No wonder the touch of her fingers made his blood fizz.

"How do you square doing what you do with being a Christian, Dad?"

Karl van Jennions shook his head as if the answer was obvious. "Friedman, the trouble with turning the other cheek is that the guy hits that too, and probably some other guy's as well – like the bully in the playground. You've surely heard of the concept of the just war? War's wrong, but sometimes it's a guy's duty to go to war to prevent a greater wrong. Like in 1939 to stop Hitler, and in '91 to stop Saddam Hussein when he invaded Kuwait. The USA is a big powerful country and it's our duty to go to the aid of smaller countries."

"Like Super Man?" said Olivia.

"A bit like Super Man." Her father tugged one of her pigtails. "And that's why I'll be flying off again in a day or two to keep an eye on Saddam, make sure he's staying put in his own country and isn't planning on invading some place else." He turned to Friedman. "I hope that's answered your question."

Hilde's head was full of counter arguments. Words were rushing into her head. Maeve's words. Oil. The good old USA didn't go round defending all the little countries that needed help, just countries with oil for their oversized cars. And they weren't just keeping an eye on Saddam. They were going to 'liberate' Iraq, which meant invade. Bomb enough people and you might hit Saddam. Was that fair? Is that what the Iraqi people wanted? Had anyone asked them? Would it stop terrorism or provoke it? She glanced at Friedman who was regarding his father thoughtfully, and then at her brother who started to address his hero like an old friend.

"Can you tell us what you do, Karl, when you fly over Iraq? I mean, some people say you're already bombing the Iraqi people." He meant Maeve and her friends. "They say the USA has been bombing Iraq for years to get rid of WMDs and they've killed Iraqis in the process."

"Well, no, Tom, we're not and we haven't. We're making sure Saddam's forces stay inside Iraq, and we're keeping a lookout for Weapons of Mass Destruction."

"And if you find any?" said Hilde.

"We've taken some out."

"Is that why the inspectors can't find any?"

"Do you ever get shot at?" said Tom.

Karl hesitated as Marty told Olivia and Cally they could leave the table if they wished and come back later for dessert. When they'd gone he said, "Let's say we're pretty good at looking after ourselves, and I should say I see myself as a peace-keeper not a warmonger. No soldier, especially not one who has seen action, likes war. In fact," – he looked straight at Hilde – "you could say I'm one of your peace weavers too, but I weave in and out of the clouds, dodging Saddam's anti-aircraft guns."

That was sick.

Frank chipped in, ""If you want peace, prepare for war," as the Romans said. Is that still viable today?"

"Sure is," said Karl. "And sometimes the threat can be enough. That's why the French veto on force was so destructive."

"No it wasn't," said Hilde. "The French want weapons inspectors to keep on looking for WMDs, and that makes sense. While they're there the Iraqis aren't using them."

Frank said, "I agree with that."

Silence. Hilde was amazed at his support. Karl and

Marty seemed embarrassed. And suddenly, glimpsing a computer in the corner of the room, Hilde had an idea.

She stood up. "Sorry, but I've got to go. If you want peace, prepare for peace. That's what I believe."

"Peace!" Tom shouted from the other side of the table. "What do you know about it? If something's peaceful, nice, like this" – he waved his hand round the table – "...you have to ruin it!"

Frank said, "Honey, Hilde, eat your meal first."

Marty said, "Karl will be giving you all a lift back."

But Hilde was already ducking under the doorway into the kitchen. "Thank you, but I'd rather walk!" And she went, through the kitchen door, knowing she hadn't got it completely right, but at least she'd made a start. Perhaps she'd get better with practice. As she closed the door she heard Friedman say he'd see she got home OK.

*

"Go away. I don't need an escort."

He caught her up by St Peter's church, where the flint chippings embedded in the stone glittered in the moonlight. The clock on the tower struck seven as they strode side by side down the street, past the bungalows and thatched cottages. Fired by her thoughts – now she knew why she kept seeing Maethilde the Peace Weaver! – she walked fast, but he kept pace with her.

"I said "Go away!"" She stopped at the crossroads. There was traffic or she'd have crossed over. The road back to the base was straight ahead. "I can find my own way back."

"I jus' wanted to say…" Gulp. "…that I respect what you say."

"Respect? What does that mean?" She glanced at his face, suddenly lit by headlights, then back at the traffic, because he was looking at her too intently.

"But my father isn't a gun-slinging redneck. Saddam Hussein is an evil dictator. He's killed and tortured thousands of people."

"I know. I'm against him too."

"The US thinks he's got to be stopped…"

"I think he's got to be stopped, but not by bombing thousands of innocent people. The cure would be worse than the disease."

"Wouldn't getting rid of him make the world safer?"

"Would it?" She pointed to the war memorial on the other side of the road. "World War 1. Millions dead. Do you think that was necessary?"

He didn't know enough to answer.

"It wasn't, and it caused World War II. Hitler wanting revenge."

"I just know, Dad says the US and the UK want to use the threat of war to make Saddam hand over his WMDs to prevent more 9/11s."

"Really?" She looked sorry for him. "And you believe him?"

He crossed the road with her. She didn't waste her breath telling him to go. Nor did she tell him about the plan taking shape in her mind. To use the web to mobilise all the people who were against the war. Using an on-base computer to run a peace campaign was something he might feel bound to mention.

Friedman pointed to the right. "I know a shorter way back, through Gate 2. It's near the dig."

She shrugged. "OK, to the gate, but no further."

That would be excellent in fact. She could stop at the dig and put the brooch back. They walked in silence along the main road for a bit, then a winding lane for about a mile.

He resisted grabbing her hand.

She resisted breaking into a run. Her plan was SO good. She couldn't wait to begin. But that wasn't the only reason she wanted to run. She felt him fancying her, could feel the heat of his body as he walked beside her.

At last they arrived at Gate 2 which was as heavily guarded as Gate 1. When she saw Friedman reach in his pocket for his ID, she shook her head. "Go home or I'll make a scene." She was obviously convincing because he put it back and stood awkwardly. She produced hers, got the OK, and he pointed to a war memorial about a hundred metres inside the gates. "Turn right there, and then follow the path through the trees past a pond and that'll bring you to the back of the dig-site. You know the way to Frank's from there."

She felt his eyes on her as she followed his instructions, walked briskly till she felt she was out of his sight, and then broke into a run.

The area beyond the memorial was oddly rural. She'd never seen anything like it on base. Through the trees she caught glimpses of water glimmering like yellow glass, and she could hear ducks quacking. Eventually the path came out by the finds shed. Now all she had to do was cross the site, dodging the moving eyes of the CCTV cameras whose positions she knew well, put the clasp back and hurry back to Frank's. But when she felt for the clasp it wasn't there. Panic – for a moment – till she remembered she'd put clean combats on that morning. Foiled again. The combats she'd worn yesterday were back in her bedroom. Just as well perhaps. Now she could hurry back to the house and start what she had to do on Frank's computer before he and Tom got back. As she crossed the site, other skeletons caught her eye. Lots of them. The archaeologists had found the cemetery they were searching for. She stepped carefully and kept her imagination in check. But when she reached Trench 3 she more than half expected to see a girl in a blue dress lying there. But there was only a skeleton with hollow eyes and huge teeth.

"Maethilde, I've got the message. I'm going to do my best. I'm going to try and be a Peace Weaver like you."

Chapter 13

When she got back she rushed into the sitting room and logged on, not sure exactly how she was going to begin her campaign. For starters she got onto Google and typed in Peace Campaign – and immediately discovered that other people had moved faster. That a Stop the War campaign was well underway. That a huge march and demonstration was planned for February 15th. At first she felt miffed – not so original then – but that feeling changed. The web was throbbing with peace initiatives. It was thrilling that lots of people had the same idea. Peace weaving was happening. There were already petitions to sign and send on to other people.

She signed several and forwarded them to everyone she had email addresses for, mostly friends at Crosby Upper. Almost instantly a sixth former called Sadie

Marshall replied, urging Hilde to go on the march and join the Hands Up for Peace campaign, just started by pupils at a London comp. They were asking pupils all over the country to decorate a handprint with a signed message of peace and send it to them. The London campaigners were going to 'plant' the handprints in the grass outside the Houses of Parliament. Hilde got onto the Hands Up for Peace website and saw they'd already planted thousands! Why hadn't she heard about all this before? When she heard Frank and Tom returning she logged off and shot upstairs. Words were in her head, but she'd said enough for one evening. Now was the time for action.

Safe in her room she drew round her hand and printed NO BLOOD FOR OIL in red. Then she made a brick for another group's Wall of Peace. She wrote TALK NOT TANKS on that. But what else could she do? Go on the Stop the War march? She grabbed her diary. Sadie had said that only the super power of public opinion could stop a super power intent on war. They needed millions to turn up. February 15th was only a fortnight away. Something else caught her eye. Ruthie was due back from France today! Hilde rang her mobile. Texted her. PCM ☺ Hilde. Rang her home and left a message with Mrs Curtis.

"Please ask her to ring me straightaway."

Words were spinning in her head. Talk not Tanks. Words not Weapons. Dialogue not Death. She could have made a dozen banners, but got ready for bed instead, because she wanted to sleep. She wanted to dream, wanted to know about Maethilde and Manfried. What happened next? In her last dream they'd been standing at the head of their armies, facing each other across the sand. The stepmother-wife had been urging Manfried to fight. Had he obeyed?

But sleep wouldn't come. She lay tossing and turning. Keyboards not Kalashnikovs. Make love not War. Not original but... Eventually she must have nodded off, but when she woke in the morning she couldn't remember dreaming about anything.

*

When she got downstairs Frank got up to put toast in the toaster. "You must be starving, honey – and haven't you got soccer this morning?" He consulted the kitchen notice board where he tried to keep track of everyone's comings and goings, and answered himself. "Yes. Sunday. You've got a match."

Was 'starving' a reference to her hurried exit last night? No one could accuse Frank of seeking confrontation.

She said, "I'm sorry, about storming out, I mean, not what I said."

He nodded. "I told Karl and Marty a bit about your mom, and how close you are."

"I thought you wanted to keep it quiet."

"Well, you had sorta..." He stopped mid-sentence, staring at the TV on top of the fridge. It was Maeve on the Human Shield bus, which had just arrived in the Bulgarian capital. British Nurse Mother of Two had decided to face the camera this time, but obviously thought she could still keep her name secret. Hilde felt the same mix of emotions as last time – pride and panic.

But Frank was simply furious. "How could she? Why didn't she tell me? Did you know?"

She didn't answer.

"So you did? That explains a lot."

"Someone's got to do something!"

"Someone's got two kids who need her!"

"You never finished Babar!"

"WHAT?"

She rushed upstairs so he wouldn't see her crying. How dare he criticise Maeve? When he'd left his two little children. One day he was nice daddy reading to them both every night. Next he'd gone, in the middle of *Babar the Elephant*. She remembered feeling so sure he'd come back to finish it.

She heard him coming upstairs.

He knocked on her door. "Hilde. We must talk. Please let me in."

But she didn't. Couldn't.

Later, she thought of two ways of helping the Stop the War campaign. There were things she and she alone could do! Hurriedly she wrote a letter.

Dear Mum,
I do want to help Myra Jennings and the Friends with their

113

demo and I've thought of what I can do – send them my ID card. Couldn't someone who looks a bit like me use it? It would be easier than cutting through and it would make a huge impact if someone came through the main gates and put up a banner, or even placed a mock-bomb in a strategic place, to show how easy it was. I wish YOU could come. You could dye your hair and perm it! All eyes are on places like this at the moment because of troops going out to the Gulf so it would get masses of publicity.

Peace and love,

Hilde

She wrote a similar letter to Myra Jennings herself, suggesting that she and the Friends make their own protest on Whiston Base on February 15th, the day of the big demo in Hyde Park. The military wouldn't be expecting activists. They'd think they were all in London. She asked Myra Jennings to get back to her asap. If the Friends decided to synchronise with the big demo, she'd send her card straightaway, if not she'd send it later. She didn't want to let her card go sooner than necessary as she'd be trapped on base without it.

Her other idea would have to wait till she got back from soccer. It was a good job Frank had reminded her about that. It wasn't just a practice today but a match in the Sunday League and they'd be relying on her. Peace weave! It wouldn't help win their hearts and minds if she let them down. She ran all the way to the field, but as soon as she opened the locker room door she realised she needn't have bothered.

Voices stopped her in her tracks.

"Arlene's better." That was Trina.

"She doesn't know the rules."

"But she's got team spirit, not like HRH."

Then someone saw Hilde in the doorway. She turned and left straightaway, to save further embarrassment. Sylvie ran after her, caught her up by the gate, and tried to smooth things over.

"If you could just be more, well friendly, you know, hang out with people a bit more. You're so…well, secretive. Folks think you're stuck up. And why don't you come to school?"

"Because…Look. I'm sorry." Sylvie had tried hard to be friendly. So had Janey. "I'll call you OK? Give me your number, please. I'd like to explain."

Did she mean that? There wasn't time to think about it. Right now she had more important things to do.

When she got off base she phoned Ruthie, who hadn't replied to the messages she'd left last night. There was no reply this time either. She left another text message. PCM, URR Hilde ☺ Urgent was the word. If her demo on base plan went ahead, she'd need a home with Ruthie PDQ. Then she walked into Erisham to post her letters – just in case Lieutenant-Colonel van Jennions had informed the military they had a dissident in their midst. By the time she got back to Frank's it was two o'clock. Luckily he was out and so was Tom. She could get on with her other idea.

Frank had lots of technical books. She found one on setting up a website and began to create www.peace-weavers.com It took ages to enter even a little bit of info and she had lots. Frank had got her several books on the Anglo-Saxons, including one called *Peace-Weavers and Shield-Maidens*. It had gripped her from the very first page. The first Peace Weaver mentioned in history was also the first English woman ever mentioned, in 550 by a Roman called Procopius. He didn't say what her name was. Unfortunately only a fragment of what he'd written remained, but he said she was an Engle who agreed to marry a man from a different tribe so that there would be peace between their tribes, and when he tried to back down she sailed across the North Sea – leading an army – to make him keep his word. It sounded just like Maethilde!

By the time Frank and Tom came home she'd only created one page. After dinner she went back to it, but soon felt sleepy. Longing now to dream, and find out more about Maethilde and Manfried, she put the brooch under her pillow.

Waves were crashing onto the shore, getting closer by the minute, but Manfried couldn't take his eyes off the girl walking towards him now, her long legs striding forwards, her blue dress skirting the sand.

The stepmother hissed in his ear. "Foreign upstart. Bid her leave."

But he couldn't, couldn't speak to the girl who had stopped only ten paces from him. Her wondrous bluebell blue eyes were looking straight into his.

She spoke in a voice husky but clear. "My lord, I am Maethilde, your wife-man, come to take my place in your hall. I come as Peace Weaver as I promised — before the Earth Mother — when I accepted your gifts." And now she raised both forearms, turning them so that he could see the clasps on her sleeves.

"A deer for my dear.

My heart for yours."

She had understood!

"You gave me your heart, and I give you mine," she said and his heart leaped. For she had understood as he had longed for her to understand when he had made the clasps. She had read his mind as he'd longed for her to read it, when he sent his gift across the sea. She was as wise as she was beautiful. She was his chosen wife-man.

But the stepmother persisted. "Take it. Take her heart. She says it is yours. Tell her to leave or you will take it with your sword!"

He heard the thud of feet behind him, the clatter of Mercian spears.

"You are right, lady, I am his, " said Maethilde, turning to the stepmother. "Manfried pledged his troth to me when he was free

117

to pledge it, and I was free to pledge mine."

There were words unspoken, but Manfried heard them and so perhaps did Eadith the stepmother.

"You were not free and neither was he when you pledged to one another," said Maethilde, and she was right.

He and the stepmother had promised to wed while each was wed to another. So it was no promise. And it was no marriage. In the months since his father died the two had not yet shared a bed. It was against nature. He had known that from the start. It was wrong. That was why he had sent the messenger to tell Maethilde to keep his gifts. But she, as wise as she was lovely, would not have the gifts without him, for she understood their meaning. In taking them she had taken him. So what must he do now? What could he do?

Even as he thought these thoughts he heard the hiss of steel.

Chapter 14

No. Can't wake up now. Hilde kept her eyes closed, trying to shut out sounds from below. She couldn't wake up yet. Must, must know what happened next. Hiss of steel. The brooch…she felt for it under her pillow, hoping the touch of it would make the dream carry on. It couldn't stop there…

"'Bye, Dad!"

"'Bye, Tom."

The door slammed. Slammed again a few minutes later, banishing sleep. Gone. The dream had gone completely. She opened her eyes. Eight o'clock. Monday. To the site then – with the brooch.

She was the first to arrive, except for Beth who was in the office when she signed in. "Hi, Hilde! Do you mind working on your own for a bit in the tall woman's grave?"

"No. That's great."

Did she mind! Things seemed to be going her way for once.

Beth walked over with her to Trench 3 where the shape of a double bed was clear in the soil. The skeleton lay on the left hand side. Maethilde. Hilde felt sure it was her. But was anyone buried with her? She wanted to carry on looking, but Beth had other ideas. "If you could work on the skeleton today, brushing away as much soil as you can, that would be great. We'll be lifting her soon but, as you'll see, attention's shifted to the trench next to yours. They've found a horse. Look."

They turned round to look into a trench less than a metre away. It was filled with what Beth said was the ribcage of a horse. As they peered at it Sid arrived with a couple of students.

"Where there's an 'orse there's usually a rider," said Sid, "so let's get looking while the weather's good."

"Could it be the woman's horse?" Hilde asked to Beth's obvious surprise.

"That would be a first," she said, "but we'll consider it, if we don't find another body. Interesting idea, Hilde. We're sure the lady's of high status, not a queen or princess, but possibly a local chieftain's wife. Who knows? She may have visited the royal court at Sutton Hoo. That was only a day's ride away."

"Might they have visited Stow?" said Hilde, remembering what she'd seen in the sleeping house.

"More than likely. It's only a mile away as the crow flies. They might even have lived there."

That was an interesting thought.

As usual she liked working alone. Brushing gave her time to think, because she didn't have to worry too much about harming anything, and she had lots to think about. Now she wished she'd tried harder to make friends with people. Wished she hadn't fallen out with the soccer set. Wished she'd caught on to what peace weaving was about earlier. That it was personal as well as political, that it was about getting on with people and talking with them, arguing even, but constructively to find solutions. Word weaving, that summed it up, but till recently it seemed as if the word-weaving gene had missed her.

Throughout the morning shouts arose from the trench next to hers.

"Good! Fantastic!"

Then groans as a sewer was discovered going right through the mound.

"Oh no!"

But it missed the grave by ten centimetres. "Hurray!"

More cheers as human bones were discovered close to the horse's front legs. Not the woman's horse then. The horse and the man – by the end of the morning they were almost certain it was a man – had been buried close together at one end of a rectangular ditched area, an unusually large mound.

"Might there be a whole family beneath it?" someone

asked during lunch in the finds shed. They all sat at one of the long tables.

"Maybe his wife and children are at the other end?"

Everyone seemed to hope so and Hilde hoped they wouldn't. So she was still out of sync with other people, still didn't want what everyone else seemed to want, but she did manage to say, "Perhaps the tall woman" – she nearly said Maethilde – "is his wife? Perhaps he died first and was buried with his horse, and she…"

Everyone was staring as if one of the skeletons had spoken, but Meri patted her hand. "Carry on, Hilde." So she did.

"If she died later, she might have had herself buried – she must have left orders – on a double bed, ready for them both in the next life."

"Mmm," said Meri. "I like that. I like that idea very much."

Back in Trench 3 – she hurried back before the others – Hilde suddenly realised she could bury the brooch. It was the ideal opportunity at last! Quickly she unzipped the pocket, took it out, and took off the bubble wrap she'd protected it with.

Then a shadow fell over her.

"Hi." The American voice was unmistakable. "Whatcha doing?"

She plunged her hand back in her pocket…

"Alas, poor Yorick," said Friedman with a nod towards the skeleton "Did you know him?"

"It's a woman," she said.

"How do you know?"

"Her sciatic notch."

Hilde was amazed she could speak. Had he seen the brooch? Back in her pocket now, it felt warm to her fingers. And her face was burning. He was staring at her, and she was staring at him. Why couldn't she move? It was as if they were held together by invisible bonds. Something passed overhead though whether it was a bird or a jet she couldn't have said. Then another voice broke the spell.

"Don't you two want to see what we've found next door?"

Hilde wrenched her head round to see Beth and a crowd of people round the other trench. When had they turned up?

"It's very exciting. Come and see." Beth turned back to the trench behind them.

"Wanna hand?" Friedman offered his.

"NO!" She clambered out, but not before their fingers had touched and her pulse rate tripled.

As he stood next to Hilde peering at the latest find Friedman felt supercharged. It was as if electricity was flowing between them. Surely she felt it too? So far so good. He hadn't got long – about half an hour before he was due back at school – to strike up the sort of intelligent conversation she seemed to like. Tom said she read a lot, books and newspapers. Well, he read too, and he'd bought the English papers yesterday, had been surprised to find how anti-American some of them were. Why did people dislike Americans? He glanced at her profile and then at the skeleton of the horse in the trench – Beauty and the Beast! Or was he the beast?

Hilde's hand was still shaking. Had Friedman seen the brooch? Around them photographers were snapping at the horse as if they'd found Shergar. The local media had turned up in force. Journalists scribbled as Beth briefed them. The warrior and his horse were news. "Perhaps they died together in battle?" someone said excitedly. "Possibly," said Beth. She pointed out his sword. Hilde felt anger rising. Why was everyone excited about a warrior? Why was war so exciting? The Peace Weaver hadn't brought the press to the site.

Beth directed photographers to key areas.

"See how the horse's front legs are bent back as if against the solid vertical edge of the coffin and the left hind leg is raised at the ankle joint over the corner. That shows the horse was put in the grave after the coffin." She pointed to its head. "Look at the bridle, bridle fitments I should say, because the leather is long gone." She shone a torch onto the horse's skull. "That looks like gold!"

Something leaf-shaped glinted like the brooch glinted when Hilde first saw it.

"I think it's a decorative pendant," said Beth, "which

might have hung from the bridle. But why would a local chieftain have such a magnificent bridle? That's what I want to know." She turned to journalists. "Imagine the glitter when those pendants shook with the horse's movement. I wonder what colour the horse was."

Black. Hilde almost said it aloud, because as Beth spoke she saw it. The jingle of harness made her look up and there was a black horse coming towards her, diagonally across the site, led by a tall woman with red-gold hair. There were children with her, three children, two girls one boy. It was Maethilde. She was holding the little boy's hand. Hilde saw it as clearly as in her dreams, but she wasn't dreaming, unless it was some sort of daydream. It was a vision like the one she'd seen on Saturday.

"Right, back to work, everyone!" Beth shouted and people started to disperse.

Friedman touched Hilde lightly, because she didn't seem to hear Beth, didn't seem to notice his hand on her arm either, so he left it there. She was staring into the distance.

Hilde was watching the woman's sad pale face getting paler, paler, as the whole amazing scene faded.

"Recess over." Friedman risked leaving his hand for a moment longer.

Hilde was transfixed. Going going…gone. When she looked to see who'd touched her arm, she was shocked to see a dark young man. "Manfried, but…"

Friedman was surprised to find her gazing into his eyes.

"Why'd you call me...?"

"I said back to work, you two." Beth laughed.

Friedman turned Hilde towards the tall woman's trench. As he led her back to it he couldn't help noticing that, dazed as she seemed, her hand stayed over one of her pockets, on whatever she'd hidden so quickly when he arrived. Girl stuff he supposed. Perhaps she wasn't feeling too good? Back in the trench, he saw her zip up the pocket before picking up a brush. Reluctantly he said goodbye – and set off for school, still wondering why she'd called him Manfried.

Hilde hardly noticed him go – she was feeling too stunned by what she had seen – and she felt odd and confused for the rest of the afternoon. Having such vivid dreams at night was disturbing enough.

During tea break Beth gave out some leaflets. "It's about the new Treasure Act, which replaces earlier laws," she said and Sid laughed.

"No need to read it. The gist is we can all get three months in jail or a fine of up to five thousand pounds if we put summat in our pockets instead of handing it over."

Everyone else laughed. Hilde felt sick. Why had she taken the brooch in the first place? Why was it proving impossible to put it back? Because she didn't want to? Ruthie would have some psychological explanation for it. "Please get in touch, Ruthie!"

Later, in her bedroom, she took the brooch out of her pocket, turned it over in her hand and noticed it looked different. At first she wasn't sure why. Then she realised the little red stone in the centre had gone! She turned her pocket inside out. She searched the bedroom floor, but realised it must have fallen out earlier. And now it was dark outside. There was no point in going to look for it. So now she was a vandal as well as a thief. Jets thundered overhead. The walls shook. More bombs. Things were worsening on every front. Well, she couldn't go back to the site and start searching for the stone, but she could try even harder to be a Peace Weaver.

Frank was on late shift at the library and Tom was out with one of his many friends. The sitting room was empty and Frank's computer was free. She ran downstairs and logged on to her website. She spent the rest of the evening trying to write her Peace Weaver petition, which everything else on her website would lead up to. It took ages, partly because she looked at other petitions first, to help get the wording right. Not that she wanted hers to be like other people's. She wanted hers to be unique, not just about stopping this war, but all wars, not just about stopping war but creating peace. It wasn't easy, but she did find writing easier than talking. At least you had time to think and look up words and re-write if you didn't manage to say what you wanted first time, or second or third. At last, as she heard someone coming in through the front door, she thought she'd done her best.

Fifteen hundred years ago PEACE WEAVING was a vital strand in our culture. In early societies women, the weavers of cloth and clothes and furnishings, also wove the fabric of society. They wove words to create peace. That was their job. With skilful word weaving, kind deeds and the exchange of gifts women tried to strengthen the bonds that joined people. And men consulted them about ways of avoiding blood feuds and battles. Even then, some people saw that war was a waste of society's most precious resource, people.

We, the undersigned, men and women, young and old, want to build on this tradition. We urge governments to create the fabric of society in all countries of the world. We urge them to resolve differences by discussion and strengthen bonds between people by fair trade and helping those in need, by building houses and hospitals, schools and libraries, farms and factories, theatres and concert halls so people can enjoy life. Peace is living without fear. We call upon governments to desist from war and use the billions of pounds spent on arms on PEACE WEAVING.

She signed her own name, logged off, said a quick goodnight to Frank and Tom, and hurried upstairs. When she went to bed, she put the brooch under her pillow, pulled the duvet over her head, and heard waves surging almost before her eyes were closed.

The tide was coming in fast, swirling into the estuary. Waves crashed and seabirds screeched as Maethilde faced Manfried across the darkening sand. "I am yours," she said again.

"And I am yours!" He breathed the words as he laid down his sword and took off his helmet.

"What are you doing?"

He ignored the stepmother's words.

The wind dropped. Silence. Even the seabirds seemed to listen. Maethilde could see his face now — and the stepmother's. She looked furious, and must have heard the words which filled Maethilde with joy.

I am yours!

They had come sooner than she had hoped, and before she had set up the loom on which to weave peace with the stepmother. And now there were murmurings and mutterings from the Mercian henchmen around her.

She must act quickly. "My Lady Eadith..."

But she was not quick enough.

Hiss!

Maethilde saw the arrow only as some sixth sense made Manfried raise his shield and catch it on the edge. Watchers gasped as the arrow — heading straight for her — trembled on the rim of his shield. Most didn't see Edgar, Eadith's eldest son, draw his sword and lunge towards Maethilde. But Manfried did. Grabbing his sword, he brought it down hard on Edgar's, but Edgar held onto the hilt, and turned now on Manfried, lunging for his chest but meeting shining shieldboss, as in a single movement Manfried lowered his shield and lunged his own sword at the stepbrother. And in it slid, in it glided through the leather lower half of his shield, and further till it stopped as blade hit bone. Blood spurted from the stepbrother's skewered body, but still he jabbed, still he stabbed his sword at Manfried who parried as best he could, while trying to wrench his own sword free. And when at last he did, it came out in a gushing fountain of blood, and the stepbrother staggered forward then fell to the ground with dreadful, tortured groans.

What price peace now? Manfried feared the worst as the stepmother fell on her knees beside her son, who was still writhing and retching blood.

A black stain spread on the sand.

"STAY BACK!" To Manfried's relief Engles and Mercian troops alike heeded his words, though the latter were looking at Eadith as if awaiting orders. But she was kneeling by Edgar's body, watching his blood seep into the sand.

Maethilde moved to her side as the older woman lifted the bloody head onto her lap with tears running down her furrowed face.

Grey hair mingled with gold as Maethilde spoke. "Do we want more of this, lady? Or can we find a way to weave a peace in which we all may thrive?"

Chapter 15

Blood was spreading across the sand. Black. She was drowning in blackness ... blood on sand ...

"Do we want more of this?"

"No!" Hilde's own shout woke her in the middle of the night, pulling her out of her dream. But next morning the image of blood on sand was still there, wouldn't go away, though other details had faded. Blood on sand. Was it a premonition? It filled her with urgency. What else could she do to help stop the war before more blood was shed? She thought of her mum, of bombs raining on Baghdad, shattering bodies, blowing limbs sky high. Don't think of Maeve. YES, think of Maeve and the people she was with. Face the facts. That was the point they were trying to make, that thousands of people like them would die or be maimed if the war went ahead. Downstairs a door banged.

"'Bye, Dad!"

"See ya, Tom!"

Frank came upstairs and knocked on her door.

"Hilde, what are you doing today?"

"Going to the site." To look for a tiny red stone she didn't say.

When the house went quiet she got up. Logged on to her website. Twenty-five hits already! While she'd been sleeping, people all over the world, mostly in America, had been signing up for peace. As she set off she felt unusually optimistic.

Beth and Sid arrived at the dig at the same time as she did and walked over to Trench 3 with her.

"What do you reckon?" Beth consulted Sid as they stood admiring the tall woman's ribcage, now fully exposed. "Hilde may be an amateur, but I think she's got a real talent for this. Can we risk letting her start lifting and boxing the lady?"

"There's no one else free," said Sid, "and we're running out of time."

As he went off to get plastic boxes and acid free paper, Beth explained what Hilde would have to do. She gave her a pad of squared paper. "You'll have to keep records as well, remember, use the grid and plot the position accurately. I'd start with the hand and arm nearest you, if I were you."

It was good working alone, even if it was because the

warrior was getting all the attention. She was able to keep a lookout for the stone, which she was sure she must have dropped when she was trying to hide it from Friedman. The search for the stone made slow work even slower. There were so many tiny bones in a hand. By the end of the day, she hadn't found the stone and she'd only boxed the hands and a lower arm. Beth seemed pleased though, and Hilde felt even more optimistic. She'd had another idea – for something else she could do to help the Stop the War campaign – steal, or rather borrow, the Peace Weaver skeleton.

But was it a good idea and could she make it work? One drawback was that Beth kept looking in to check on her work, and Beth took what she'd boxed up to the finds shed. But maybe tomorrow she'd have more time to herself?

"It'll be mad here," Beth said as they were all getting ready to leave in the evening. "The national press are coming, and the British Museum's Anglo-Saxon expert. Everyone's so excited by this latest find."

It was the same old story, thought Hilde. A warrior was Big News. A Peace Weaver was No News. But that situation might help her to do what she wanted to do.

It didn't. Mad was the word for the frenzy on site next morning. When Hilde arrived camera crews and reporters were already jostling for position round the warrior's grave; there were cables all over the ground, and she couldn't get near the Peace Weaver's trench, which was covered by planks.

"Sorry. It's to stop people trampling all over it," Beth said before carrying on talking to the bearded man by her side. It was a famous archaeologist who presented TV programmes. Hilde picked up that the warrior was going to be on the national news that evening, and that there might be a whole programme about him. She went to the office to find Sid and ask him what she could do.

He seemed surprised she wanted to work, but sent her to a newly-opened trench when she said she didn't want to just hang around. Soon she saw Friedman's father turn up with more military personnel, and a class of High School kids, Friedman's class. She kept her head down, but it wasn't long before he was peering down at her.

"Don't you wanna be on TV with everyone else?"

The rest of his class were gawping at the warrior or sucking up to his dad.

"Waving at Mother you mean? Sticking my tongue out?"

He laughed. "Why're you so mad?"

"Because everyone thinks a warmonger is more important than a peace weaver."

"Didn't your lady have weapons?"

"Defensive weapons."

But now one of the women was shushing her, and another was introducing Friedman's father. The site went quiet.

"Lieutenant-Colonel Karl van Jennions III, may I ask

for your thoughts about the warrior in front of you?"

He pushed his cap to the back of his head. "Proud. Yes, that's the word. Proud that the USAF is supporting this project, proud yes, to be part of a military tradition on this piece of land, stretching back for over fourteen hundred years, and sorta proud that this guy seems to have been a good guy." He nodded as if agreeing with himself, and then turned towards Beth. "And now on behalf of Airborne Division I'd just like to wish you and your team the very best of luck in your endeavours. I hope you find out even more, 'cos I'd sure like to know what this fella did to earn that magnificent bridle, how he used that amazing sword. I'll certainly be looking in on you later, might even become one of your volunteer workers, but right now duty calls. I've gotta be off. So thank you, thank you all, very much."

There was a flurry of applause, during which Friedman told Hilde that his dad had majored in history. Then the reporter started to interview an arms expert from the British War Museum who said that the steel sword was top of the range, the latest technology in the sixth century, the equivalent of today's F-15 fighter jet.

"The sword-maker must have been a highly skilled craftsman. The Anglo-Saxons were great craftsmen."

"And women," hissed Hilde. "Why are swords more interesting than spindles, spears more interesting than weaving battens? If it hadn't been for women they'd all have run round starkers, their houses would have been

135

freezing and they'd have starved to death."

Friedman beat a hasty retreat, the better to advance later, he told himself, and went to see his father. Caught him up as he was climbing into his truck.

"Good talk, Dad. Not too long."

"Thanks, son."

They'd said goodbye earlier, the whole family had, back in Pyghtle Cottage. It had been a bit tense to say the least. His dad was starting a mission to the Gulf that day. Didn't know when he'd be back.

"'Bye then."

"'Bye, son." Karl started the engine and Friedman was about to walk away when the engine died, and his dad got down from the truck and surprised him with a hug, a big bear hug, like when he was a kid. "Look after your mom and sisters, Friedman. Remember, you're the big man while I'm away."

"Sure."

Hilde watched them hugging. Blood on sand. Her dream returned and something froze in her. They seemed to be in slow motion and she wanted to cry, "Don't go!" But they were already pulling away from each other.

Now the lieutenant-colonel was driving off, without a backward glance, and Friedman was rejoining his classmates.

She left early, disgusted by all the fuss round the warrior's grave. At six o'clock that night, she was in the kitchen when Frank switched over to the BBC news. Most of it was about Iraq. Weapons inspectors weren't finding WMDs. More troops were going out to the Gulf. Tony Blair was rushing round Europe trying to get backing for a UN resolution backing an invasion. But – Hilde was pleased to see – the Stop the War movement was gaining momentum. The demo was going to take place in Hyde Park. The government had refused permission at first, but public opinion had forced them to change their minds. There was no mention of the dig.

"'Spect it'll be on the local news," Frank said.

She'd told him what had been happening on site.

But Anglia News was about the Stop the War campaign too. Lots of local people were going to London for the march. There were interviews with some of them, and it looked as if the Anglo-Saxon warrior had been held over. But then the newsreader's tone lightened. "There was more excitement today at the Whiston USAF Base, where archaeologists are excavating an Anglo-Saxon cemetery. Two very old skeletons are proving particularly interesting."

"Two?" said Frank. "I thought you said they were only interested in one of them?"

"Two," said Beth from the TV screen, as if she was answering him. "Two fascinating graves, a male and a female's and an intriguing link between them."

A camera homed in on Trench 3.

Hilde couldn't believe it.

"Here we have a female with male artefacts, a shield and a sword, though the sword may have been adapted for use as a weaving batten. And over here," – the camera moved with her – "we have a male, a warrior's grave, with typical male artefacts – and a horse which is very rare – but also, very unusually this male grave contains a sleeve clasp, and they were worn only by women."

When did they find that? Now Hilde regretted leaving early.

"And the link?" prompted the interviewer.

"We've found a similar sleeve clasp in the grave of the woman," said Beth.

The camera zoomed in on a three-part clasp

Not similar, identical. Hilde nearly spoke aloud. It was the pair of the one in her pocket.

Friedman, watching TV with his mother and sisters, back at Pyghtle Cottage, hoped that Hilde was watching. Now maybe she'd stop looking at him as if were a jerk. If only she'd stayed to see that he'd noticed the clasp in the guy's grave. He'd told Beth. He'd helped to lift the planks off the woman's grave when Beth had realised the connection. He'd told the producer that the skeleton was a Peace Weaver.

Hilde went up to her room. She needed to think. The clasps in both graves – didn't that prove her dreams had been telling the truth?

There was a knock on her bedroom door a few

minutes later. When she opened it Frank handed her a book.

"Thought you might like this." He'd taken to bringing her new ones to review for him. She thought it was his way of making her work while she wasn't going to school, which he seemed to have stopped arguing about. "Like your website, by the way," he added as he turned to go downstairs.

Like your website. She tried to recall his tone of voice as he said it. Sarcastic? Angry? Had he meant it? How had he found it?

She asked him later when she went down to get a drink. He was getting a beer from the huge fridge.

"Sure I meant it. I signed your petition. Signed several. Have a look."

"You're for peace, then?"

"Honey, Hilde, most everyone's for peace. The question is how to achieve it and," he hesitated, "Americans are as divided about that as anyone else. Don't stereotype."

Feeling ticked off, she leafed through a book on the table, *Anglo-Saxon Women*.

"Got it for Beth," he said, "but you'd like it I think. It shows women had high status in Anglo-Saxon times. You know the word woman comes from wife-man meaning a weaving person? "Man" meant "person". So a wife-man was a person in her own right. Sorry. Etymology's one of my interests, but maybe your mom would like the word "wife" more if she knew a wife wasn't just an add-on to a man."

139

Maeve hated the word wife. It was amazing that she'd married anyone really. Frank looked thoughtful, but things he'd said earlier made her want to keep him talking. "If wife-man meant woman, what was the word for a man?"

He laughed. "Weapon-man, which, would you believe it, shortened to were-man – as in were-wolf?" He threw back his head and howled and she laughed. "Maybe that was why she went off me."

"I thought you went off her."

He squashed the can.

"I'd like to hear your side of things."

They sat down and he flicked the book's pages. "I was out of work. There was a lot of unemployment at the time. I couldn't get a library job, anywhere, except in the States, but Maeve wouldn't go to the States. So I…"

"Good old Mum," said Tom, going straight to the fridge. They hadn't heard him come in. "Break up the family rather than join the evil empire."

"Because she has principles!"

"But what are they?" said Tom with a mouthful of pizza.

"Steady on, you two." Frank got up. "I left, I gotta own up to that, because I didn't want to live on welfare. I gotta job here on the base, thinking, hoping she'd accept that compromise, temporarily at least, but she couldn't."

"Wouldn't," said Tom.

Later, as she lay in bed, Hilde felt even more confused.

140

Grey smoke spiralled up to the sky roof from the funeral pyre on the other side of the river. Maethilde watched it from the doorway of the hall at West Stow. Saw her brother waiting near the weaving house, with the dogs.

She turned to the older woman by her side and spoke gently, seeking the right words. "You need not leave us, stepmother."

Poor lady, in less than a year she had lost husband and son.

"Stay, I beseech you, here with your own hall and herd," Maethilde continued. "I have heard tell that you are a weaver of renown, famed for weaving fine cloth with wool from your black-faced sheep — and for your peace weaving in former times. Manfried says that for seven long years you wove peace between Mercian and East Engle."

The woman seemed to be listening though she did not take her eyes from the spiralling smoke.

"Should we not strive to keep that peace, not tear holes in it? And can we not make a firmer, richer fabric by weaving into it another strand? Cannot Mercian, New Engle and Old live in harmony? Stay — with your own hall and serving women — in the settlement of Manfried and myself for as long as you wish. I have much to learn and will need a mother's guidance while I take my place here."

May Wyrd make them the right words, and give her the wisdom to live in peace with the stepmother!

"Manfried too, he wishes you to stay," she said as her husband stepped into the hall. "Is that not right, Manfried?"

He nodded and Maethilde went on. "I brought you a gift, lady. My brother..." She beckoned Edwin to come forward. "He also has a herd of sheep, though their wool is not as soft as from yours and he has dogs to guard and keep them together. Look."

141

"I have dogs..."

"But not, I think, with skills like these," said Maethilde as Edwin came in, a dog with two eager pups at his heels. At a word from him they sat at his feet.

"We heard, lady, that your flock were of a wandering skittish nature, and that you have lost some of them to wolves. Are those yours there?" She pointed to the meadow, this side of the river where sheep were dotted about. "Come. Let Edwin show you what his dog can do."

The woman hesitated, then Manfried and Maethilde each took an arm and she walked with them to the meadow.

"The dog looks like a wolf itself," the stepmother said as, belly close to the grass, the dog circled the enclosure. But when only a few minutes later, all the sheep were in the wicker fold she looked impressed.

"The pups are yours if you wish," said Maethilde. "My brother will stay here to train them to look after your herd."

Edwin handed her a pup. "He will be fierce in his defence of your herd, yet gentle in their care. His mother has saved many a lamb from the wolf's jaws." The stepmother stroked the pup's silky ears and looked up at Edwin, then at Manfried. 'The young man will stay, you say?"

"For as long as you wish, Eadith. As manprice," said Manfried as Edwin nodded. "He has agreed. There is a price to pay for the loss of Edgar."

No one said — even though it was Edgar's own fault.

"And Edwin will pay it willingly," said Maethilde.

"My father wanted peace," said Manfried.

"You two," said the stepmother, "you sing a good song together."

Chapter 16

Hilde woke with a hopeful feeling – Maethilde and Manfried had got together! – even though the window-panes were rattling and there was a distant whine of jets overhead.

When she got downstairs, Frank handed her a letter with a Bulgarian stamp.

"From your mom? Let's hope she's on her way back."

"I'll tell you later."

She went upstairs to read it. Maeve wasn't on her way back. She'd got someone who was, to post the letter for her.

Dearest Hilde ... brilliant idea ... proud of you ... Do send your ID card to Myra...

Hilde glowed with praise.

As you may have seen – the media cover is excellent! – we are parked in a square in the middle of the city. If the so-called Coalition want to bomb Baghdad they've got to bomb us!...

The warm glow faded. Now she was scared – and frustrated. She wanted to do everything she could to stop the bombs falling, but she couldn't send the ID card yet. Myra Jennings hadn't replied, hadn't said if her group was coming on February 15th or on any other day. And if she sent her card now, without knowing, she'd be trapped on base and wouldn't be able to go on the Hyde Park demo herself, not if she wanted to return to the base, and she did – to stage her own Peace Weaver demo.

She set off for the site, hoping action would staunch her mounting fear for Maeve. There was so much to do, keep an eye out for the stone, put back the brooch if she was lucky enough to find it, and most importantly – if she was going to put her new plan into action – see if Beth objected if she, Hilde, took the pieces of skeleton to the finds shed herself. The less Beth saw of the boxes the better because – if her plan worked – there wouldn't be any bones in them.

Friedman, already in Trench 3, saw her arrive. He'd got there early to see her before he went to school and had got permission from Beth to remove the planks covering the trench. He had the last one above his head, when he saw Hilde striding towards him – and his heartbeat tripled. Had she seen the news last night? What would she say when she found out he had persuaded the BBC producer to look at the Peace Weaver's grave? He longed to tell her. Correction – he longed for someone else to tell her, so he could be self-effacing in the British way, earning her gratitude, her respect, her...

"Hello. Shouldn't you be at school?"

She didn't even look at him, just started work near the skeleton's head.

"Shouldn't you?"

Hilde was dismayed to see him there, had to get him out of the way. Had to get on.

"How do you feel about your father killing people?"

"Excuse me?"

"Your dad. Dropping bombs. Killing people. How do you feel about it?"

Some pacifist. She picked fights like some folk picked their noses.

"He'll have to, you know. That's what it means being in the military. Obeying. Losing your right to choose. And they'll be shooting at him with weapons we sold him – to keep in with Saddam because we wanted his oil."

"What about Kosovo then?" If she wanted a fight she could have one. He'd got himself better informed since the last bout. "What about '93 when the US defended the Moslems from the Serbs?"

No answer. Not so clever then.

'Was that about oil? I don't think so. Saddam has WMDs. He's supplying terrorists. He could use them against anyone. He's a dictator who tortures his own people. My d…"

But he couldn't finish. She had no idea! She should have been in their house this morning. His mother's brightness at breakfast may have fooled his sisters. It hadn't fooled him. Deep breath. Try again.

"My father is risking his life to make the whole world a safer place."

"By dropping bombs on my mum!"

"What?"

But she couldn't go on. Feeling for a tissue to blow her nose, she didn't realise she'd pulled something else from her pocket, and dropped it on the side of the trench, till she saw it shining in Friedman's hand.

"How'd you get this?" At first he thought it was part of the sleeve clasp he'd seen in the warrior's grave yesterday. Then he remembered she'd gone home before they found it, and her face was burning. She hadn't answered and he remembered her hiding something before. She looked guilty.

Hilde saw Beth and Sid coming towards them. "Give it to me, please."

He kept it in his hand.

"Hi there," said Beth. Sid grunted. He had a pile of plastic boxes under his chin.

"Friedman," said Beth, "are you going to help Hilde dismantle her ladyship? Have you told her what you found yesterday?"

"Sure I'll help." He waited a moment to see if Hilde was going to mention the brooch, and slipped it into his pocket when she didn't. He took the boxes from Sid. "Let's get going," he said, and Beth and Sid walked off. He heard Beth saying something about a lovers' tiff.

"Please give it to me. It isn't what you think." She was pleading.

"You don't know what I think."

She didn't, that was the trouble. Nor did he, though certain facts seemed obvious. "How highly principled you are."

"It isn't the one they found yesterday, though it's like it, identical I think. They're a pair. I found the one you've got here. There." She pointed a trowel at the skeleton stretched in front of them. "On my first day. Near her wrist – and I picked it up. Don't know why, except that in some weird way it seemed to belong to me. So I did and I've been trying to put it back ever since."

Her tone was matter of fact, expressionless, compared to when they'd been arguing. Her dramatics then had annoyed him. Tears, like Olivia when she thought it would get her out of trouble. Though she'd swept them away pretty quick.

They'd taken Hilde by surprise too. Suddenly all her defences had dropped – and now she'd told him stuff he'd hold against her. But if she hadn't told him he'd think she was a common thief. "I kept trying to put it back, but things, you for one, kept stopping me, not that I'm blaming you – and then I lost the garnet and now it's too late in a way, because..."

"Why didn't – don't – you just tell Beth?"

She shrugged.

"She might understand."

"Do you?" She looked straight at him.

"Dunno. Have you told anyone else?"

She shook her head.

"What were you saying – about your mom – before?"

"She's in Iraq, in Baghdad living near Iraqi people, so your dad could kill her."

Shit.

"Not just her of course. That's the point she's trying to make, that people dropping bombs don't think about what those bombs are doing on the ground. They don't think about people." She bit her lip.

Friedman's mobile rang, just as well. Double shit. There was nothing to say. This ruined everything. Harley Todd wanted to know where the hell he was? School was starting.

"I'm on my way," he lied, because he wasn't, yet. He put his phone in his pocket and got the brooch out.

"Pretty." It lay in the palm of his hand. "If that's the word." He could see that it was a fine piece of work; it looked like gold cords twisted together in a pattern. Worth a bit. He felt her watching him. It must be the pair of the one he'd found yesterday. It was exactly the same, though there was a stone missing from the middle of this one. He looked at it from another angle, and now he saw something he hadn't noticed then, the figure of a man in a tall hat and a long cloak. Cool.

She said, "He gave it – both of them – to her."

"He – this guy?" He thought she meant the man in the hat. She didn't know what he was on about, even when he pointed it out, keeping it in his hand so she had to lean close to look. He could smell the scent of her hair. Apples.

"No, I mean the warrior, in the grave." She nodded towards the other trench, and then back to the brooch. "A deer for his dear? Can't you see the deer?"

He couldn't see it, even when she turned it up the other way. Typical. Neither of them could see what the other saw. His phone rang again. He switched it off putting the brooch in his pocket at the same time.

"See ya." He stepped out of the trench and walked off, not sure what he was going to do.

*

Hilde watched him stop and talk to Sid before leaving the site, and spent the next hour expecting someone to come and accuse her of stealing. But no one came by, and no one stopped her when she took a box of bones to the finds shed. Amy was at the computer cataloguing something else.

"We're putting Trench 3's contents over there," she said pointing to a trestle table near the door, and that was all. She didn't check what was inside the box. Good.

It was eleven o'clock when Beth did come, and only to tell her to take a break. She said Friedman was coming back after school. So that's what he must have told Sid. But would he bring the brooch back? Would he give it to her?

During the break Hilde went for a wander in the trees behind the finds shed. People sometimes did on fine days. No one thought it was odd. But there was no one else there today thank goodness. As she filled her backpack with sticks and stones she wondered what Friedman would do with the brooch. He must think she was a thief. What are riches without honour? Maethilde's words in her head made her hesitate for a moment. Was she doing the right thing? Surely the cause justified what she doing? The Stop the War campaign had to succeed.

"You don't mind helping, do you, Maethilde?" Back in the trench, she was glad no one could hear her talking to a skeleton. Then checking that the CCTV camera's roving eye wasn't on her, she replaced an upper arm bone with a stick of similar size, and set off to the finds shed. Once again Amy didn't check. And if she did – before Hilde had carried out the second part of her plan, her own Super Spectacular Peace Weaver Skeleton demo! – well, just being caught might get some publicity for the cause.

Chapter 17

Friedman was late for school. He had to sign in at the office and go straight to class on the fourth floor.

Harley had kept him a place in English. "What kept ya?"

"Stuff." He didn't want to discuss Hilde with Harley who had the sense to shut up. Why were girls so difficult? He moved his chair forward, out of reach of Trina the Midget, who was trying to touch him up with her foot.

Mr Jansch looked pained. "Trina, Friedman, can Mr Thoreau have your attention?"

He tried to focus on 'Walden Pond', but Henry David Thoreau's wanderings in the woods weren't riveting.

Even ball practice during lunch didn't take his mind

151

off Hilde, especially as Tom was at the field. Did the kid know his mother was in Iraq? If he did, he didn't seem worried. He played well, was one of the best in the team now. And he'd made lots of friends, because he was a friendly outgoing kid with a positive attitude. Unlike…

After school Friedman ran all the way home to clear his head. Too bad that he'd told Sid he'd go back to the dig, but the hairy guy hadn't taken that much notice. He needed to think what to do with the brooch. Hilde Browne a thief, well that was a surprise. Fortunately no one else was home, he realised as he let himself in with his key – and when he stepped inside it was more obvious. The cottage was super clean and had that special stillness that it had when there was no one in. His mom must have taken the girls some place. When his dad was away flying she worked double time to keep occupied, cleaned the house, worked in the garden, planned even more trips out. She always had done, but he'd only recently realised why. That was women he guessed. They had their own way of doing stuff.

He waited till he was in his own room before he got the brooch out from his pocket. Then he folded himself into the window seat, keeping well back so passers-by in the street below couldn't see him. Birds scratched and twittered in the thatch and women and children's voices floated up from below. In the background aircraft rumbled hidden by cloud. On a good day you could see for miles from this window –

except where the church tower blocked the view – to the sea if your eyesight was good enough and his was. He could see the radomes on the airfield even today, and he hoped his sight stayed good – so he could join up and fly which is what he'd wanted for as long as he could remember. Posters of aircraft covered the sloping walls of his room. By the side of his bed was a photo of his dad and granddad together, and another of his great-granddad who'd been killed on D-day. Granddad and Great-Granddad had given their lives for their country.

Anger propelled him to his feet. Hilde Browne was wrong! What if the Allies hadn't fought Hitler? She wouldn't be able to hold the opinions she had now, nor would her mother. And Saddam was a Fascist like Hitler. What sort of women's rights – or men's rights – did he allow? Not doing anything about him would be like not doing anything about Hitler – even if you knew he'd gassed thousands of Jews.

"We know Saddam has gassed thousands of Kurds. Surely it's right to stop him before he does any more harm?"

Catching sight of himself in the mirror – talking to himself! – he sat on the bed to calm down. But Hilde could sweat. He hoped she was worrying about what he was going to do. He switched on the lamp to see the thing better, because away from the small window most of his attic room was in shadow. The brooch glimmered in the pool of light.

Why had he brought it home? He should have just handed it in. Now he could be accused of handling stolen property! What had Hilde said? She'd tried to put it back lots of times, but in some weird way it seemed to belong to her. Pathetic. If she'd wanted to give it back she'd have done it. But...be fair...he'd wanted to give it to Beth and here it was. Equally pathetic. He was as bad as her if he thought he couldn't give it back. He'd go to the site tomorrow, give her one more chance to give it back herself – because he didn't want to be a snitch – yes, that's why he hadn't done it before, but if she didn't...Now he caught sight of it in the pool of light beneath the lamp, caught sight of the little man with his long beard and a pointed hat, and long flowing robes, furling round his feet. Why had she said it had a deer's face? It looked nothing like a deer. If anything it was a wizard, though maybe he'd seen *Lord of the Rings* one time too many. Amazing though to think it was hundreds, more than a thousand years old. It must be valuable, even more valuable if she hadn't lost the stone in the middle. What a clown. How much was it worth? He picked it up to feel the weight of the gold in the palm of his hand, and something caught his eye, a face, a deer's face.

A deer for my dear.

My heart for yours!

His heart leaped as the words came into his head.

Hilde was feeling edgy. As she was about to make

another trip to the finds shed with a plastic box labelled RIGHT FOOT Beth arrived, on one of her inspection tours.

"I'll take that if you like. I want to see Amy."

"No it's OK." Hilde stretched. "My back needs a rest. I've been bending all day." She carried on, hoping Beth wouldn't think her rude or odd.

Amy was entering data into the computer as usual, but she got up when she saw Hilde. "As you can see I've moved things round a bit. I've put the Trench 3 finds on a smaller table."

It was closer to her computer. Was she about to start cataloguing them? If so the game was up.

Amy said, "Most of the artefacts, the sword and shield boss have gone to the lab for cleaning and analysis, and the heavier shoulder brooches. The sleeve clasps have gone to the British Museum, so we're just keeping the skeleton here."

To Hilde's relief she went back to the computer and didn't check what was in the box she'd brought from her trench. She just said, "You have labelled inside the box as well as outside, haven't you? It might be a while before we have time to examine the contents."

Hilde breathed more easily, and went back to Trench 3 feeling more confident that her plan would work – if Friedman didn't shop her first.

Back at Pyghtle Cottage Friedman ran down the narrow stairs. He'd showered. He'd changed. He'd after-shaved. Now he wanted to see Hilde, to tell her he'd seen the deer and get her to look at it the other way, to see if she could see the weird guy that he'd seen. It just goes to show there are two ways of looking at things, he imagined himself saying, their faces close together. Could we agree to differ? Respect each other's point of view? He liked the sound of that. He'd also apologise for implying she'd stolen deliberately and tell her about the time he'd taken a few dollars from his mom's purse – or maybe he wouldn't, but he'd show her, somehow, that he understood, and offer to go with her to tell Beth, or help her discover the brooch accidentally. Anything. I'll do whatever you want because I...

But the front door opened before he got to it.

"Hi, Mom! Just going..." Words died on his lips. She looked terrible. And the base chaplain was with her, his arm round her shoulders, as if holding her up. And the CO's wife was close behind holding the girls' hands. The girls were crying.

Something terrible had happened.

"Let's All Sit Down, Friedman. We've Had Very Bad News." The chaplain spoke as if every word began with a capital letter. "You're Going To Have To Be Brave."

Chapter 18

It wasn't till mid-morning next day that Hilde learned that Friedman's father had died. She was on site in Trench 3 when Beth told her, and in her mind's eye she saw Friedman hugging his dad only the day before yesterday. It was a slow motion picture like action replay. Blood on sand. Had she known something like this was going to happen?

Beth said, "Go to Friedman, if you like, Hilde. Leave now. Tell him how sorry we all are. He'll need his friends."

Friends? What made Beth think they were friends? She'd always argued with him, had argued when they'd last met. But she had to go to him. She didn't want to go, but some force stronger than want, stronger than dread – because she did dread meeting him – seemed to be pulling her. She didn't know what she'd say or do when she got there, but she had to go.

"Would you like a lift?" Beth was still there. "I can give you one myself, or shall I ring Frank?"

"No. No thanks. I'll walk." She needed the time to think about what she'd say. What she feared most for her mum had happened to his dad. What must he be feeling? Should she apologise for what she'd said yesterday? How do you feel about your dad killing people? He'll be shot at you know, with weapons we sold Iraq. Again she remembered watching them hug for the last time. For the last time.

An hour later, knocking on the door of the silent cottage, still not knowing what to say, she had a sudden urge to run away. But an old man opened it just before she could. A grumpy old man, or maybe a very upset old man. He had a packet of Go-Cat in his hand and a ginger cat was rubbing round his legs.

"Yes?"

"I've come to see Friedman."

He hesitated. "Haven't you heard?"

"Yes. I've come to say I'm sorry."

He nodded. "Well, I'm from next door, just feeding the cat," he said gruffly. "Keeping an eye on things. Mrs van Jennions and the family flew back to the USA this morning, to await the return of the lieutenant-colonel's body. The Americans bury their war dead at home. Didn't you know that? Well, I suppose there's no reason

158

why you should."

War dead? But it hadn't started yet.

He started to close the door. "If there's nothing else?"

She said no and he closed it.

Gone. Friedman had gone, so she might never see him again. Why was that devastating? She walked back in a daze. When she got to Frank's it was late afternoon, almost dark. And when she opened the front door all she could hear was 'Looney Tunes', blaring out of Tom's bedroom. Frank was coming down the stairs.

He studied her face. "You obviously know. So does Tom, but he doesn't want to talk about it, to me anyhow. You might try."

Tom's door was closed. She knocked and opened it. He was on the bed watching cartoons. She ventured in and he turned on her.

"You didn't even like him!" His face was wet.

"I disagreed with him, but I didn't want this to happen. I disagreed with him because I didn't want this to happen." Why else would she feel this ache for someone she hardly knew? She turned the TV down. "Let's go buy a card or something." She wanted to do something, anything. Couldn't sit still.

He exploded and turned the TV back up. "What's the point? What's the bloody point?"

But when she mentioned it to Frank he said he thought a sympathy card was a good idea. Before she set off for the shops she did something else which might help prevent more stupid, pointless deaths. It would be really good if Myra Jennings or one of the Friends got onto the base. Maeve was right. Do it. So she sandwiched her ID card between two pieces of cardboard, put it in an envelope and addressed it to Myra Jennings. Then she added a short letter.

Dear Myra Jennings,

I think your reply must have got lost in the post (if it hasn't been intercepted. If it has you will get arrested at the gates! Either way – good publicity! I'll make sure of that.) But I still hope you're coming on Feb 15th to synchronise with my own Peace Weaver Skeleton demo. I'm going to hang a peace weaver skeleton from a high place – with a banner of course. Here is my ID card as promised. Sorry I can't provide more than one, but if just one person gets inside it will prove how easily a terrorist or suicide bomber could do it. Good luck! Looking forward to seeing you INSIDE Whiston Base!

Peace and love,

Hilde Webster

She added her email address and mobile number.

It was dark outside – or as dark as it ever got on base – and lights were blazing in the shopping mall. A row of billboards stood outside the newspaper shop. JET CRASH IN MOUNTAIN. ENEMY ACTION OR ENGINE FAILURE? TERRORISM? THREE DEAD. PILOT AND NAVIGATORS KILLED.

Three dead already. Three unhappy families. And the war hadn't started yet. What if it went ahead? There'd be thousands. She heard someone say the jet had exploded in the sky. Saw the debris falling and thought of her mum below, but not in the mountains, thank goodness. But it was vital now to stop the war. Before bombs fell on Baghdad. She stopped at the Post Office and dropped the envelope in the mailbox. There was no time to waste. Her demo on the base, combined with the Friends' demo outside the gates, combined with one of them getting onto the base, would grab the attention of the press. She herself would tip them off. She'd have to move faster though. Dismantling, removing and reassembling the skeleton was taking longer than she'd thought. But it was the right thing to do, even though it was going to cause trouble, for herself, and yes, Frank. But, well, there were bigger things at stake.

There were no sympathy cards left. Anywhere. Karl was popular. Shop assistants hardly spoke. A few shops had closed. She walked home, the back way, so that she could call in at the dig. It was against the rules to go alone but time was short. The steps of the war memorial near Gate 2 were heaped with flowers and a teddy bear and a plastic aeroplane. Cellophane wrapping glittered in a car's headlights; the Stars and Stripes clung at half-mast and a sweet smell of flowers hung in the air.

"My dad…"

"My mum…"

Picking her way carefully along the path to the pond,

she recalled their conversation. They'd both been scared. Was that what united them?

The urge to act grew stronger. She followed the path through the trees to the dig-site. Reached the finds shed. Stopped to check there was no one around. Then keeping behind the CCTV cameras she made her way to Trench 3. Carefully she removed the left lower leg bone and put it in her backpack. Getting the larger thighbones off site was going to be harder. Making a mental note to fill a plastic box with stones next day and label it LOWER LEFT LEG, though the professionals used the proper Latin names, she hurried back to Frank's house.

He appeared as soon as she opened the front door.

She said, "Sorry, no cards left, and the van Jennions have gone back to the States by the way."

He nodded. "Maybe I'll write a letter – and here's a book, honey. We're wondering whether to buy it for the library. Might take your mind off things."

"Thanks. Goodnight."

"Goodnight, Hilde."

In her room, she glanced at the book, which was another lone heroine saves the world story. Poppy was about to be 'swept off to an alternative dimension, all the better to pursue her mission'. Lucky old Poppy. But Hilde Browne had to work in this one. Do what she could to persuade politicians to pursue peace not war, so stupid pilots wouldn't get killed on stupid so-called reconnaissance flights. On a more practical level she had

to get hold of a suitcase to take the complete skeleton –
when she'd fixed it together – to wherever she was going
to take it. Where? Where would it make maximum
impact?

"Hilde."

She jumped as Frank knocked on the door, pushed
the bag under the bed before opening up. He said he'd
found a plain card he thought might be OK and
thought about sending flowers too, if he could get the
van Jennions' American address. He said he thought
Tom would feel better if he did something, like write a
few lines. "And you, honey? I'm sure they'd like to hear
from you."

"Are you?" The words spat out, because now she was
full of doubts. Would the van Jennions, would
Friedman really want to hear from her?

*

Back home in North Carolina, in his grandmother's
house, Friedman had just gone up to the room he used
to stay in as a little kid. It had been his dad's room when
he was a boy. He could hear voices below. The house
was full of people. The chaplain had told him to look
after his mother; his dad had told him to look after his
mother, but there were plenty of people to look after her
and the girls. The three of them were cuddled together
on the sofa when he came upstairs – with a bottle of
bourbon under his sweater, because even his dad had a
glass or two after a stressful day. And he was, he'd been
told many times, 'the man of the house now'. But he

didn't feel like a man. Be brave, people said, clapping him on the back or gripping his shoulder. Be brave, be brave – that's what military families are good at. But now it took all his strength not to pick up the old teddy bear which sat on the windowsill and cry himself to sleep, because he had a pain in his chest like he'd been knifed, an ache much worse than when he'd broken a couple of ribs playing football, and only oblivion would make it go away.

But oblivion didn't come – there wasn't enough in the bottle – and the pain didn't go – it got worse. So he lay on his bed doubled up yet fully clothed because he had the feeling he ought to be ready for something.

"What?" He asked his father and his grandfather and his great-grandfather who stared, glassily, from silver frames on the wall.

"What did you do?" he asked his uniformed grandfather who had been twelve when his dad had died on D-day. He'd been told that enough times. "How were you brave?"

Then the door opened. He thought – he really did – that his dad was going to walk in, ruffle his hair and kiss him goodnight, like he did when he was a little kid. Because, because he had to be imagining this. It wasn't true. It was fear playing a trick. It had got to him at last. He waited and watched a grey cat walk in, seeking solitude from the crowd below. And now the nothing-ness that was his dad hit him. He'd never come through that door again. Never touch his hair. Never say goodnight. They'd never ever do anything together again.

As he drained the bottle he caught sight of the brooch in a pool of light on the table beside his bed, where he'd emptied his pockets earlier. The deer was looking at him. Dear heart. Hurt heart. Broken heart. He turned it round and there was the magician. "Magic him back, why don't you?"

He was drunk, he knew he was, such stupid words were coming out of his mouth as he hurled the bottle across the room, and then he was sobbing into the pillow like a baby.

"Alas for the mailed warrior.
Alas for the splendour of my best friend!"

Head held high, though tears flowed, Maethilde led the horse across the greensward — to the grave where her lord lay waiting. Why, why had the gods taken him so suddenly? Why had Wyrd snapped the thread of his life? Only two days ago he'd been her strong and upright lord, honoured by the king with splendid gifts. Then came the marsh fever striking him low in less than a day. Her herbs and tender care had been to no avail.

Alas for the mailed warrior, peace weaver and friend!

Father and lusty lover!

In her right hand was the horse's jewelled bridle, a gift from the king for honours won. With her other she held her son's hand. On his other side walked his two sisters, each of them holding a platter of roast meat for their father on his journey to the next life. Young Manfried, he carried a bucket of oats for the horse, whose white breath plumed in the frosty air as its muffled hooves moved forward to the sound of a single drumbeat.

Boom...

Boom...

Boom...

Gold and silver glittered against the warm black cheeks of the beast. How she envied it its fate, for the blow would come quickly, he would lie with his lord and together they would journey to the Great Hall in the Sky. But when would she clasp her dearest dear again? When would she lie warm in his arms and feel his sweet breath on her skin?

Alas for the mailed warrior!

Peace fighter, peace keeper!

Alas for the splendour of my best friend!

Boom...

Boom...

For seventeen years they had sung their song together, beneath the arching sky roof of East Engleland. For seventeen years they had kept the peace, in their hall and settlement and with neighbours near and far, weaving bonds of friendship. For seventeen fleeting years they had woven a tapestry of peace, rich and colourful, with strands from many tribes. Britons, Romano-Britons, Franks, Frisians, Mercians and Engles Old and New had lived in harmony — and for this great task the king had given his gifts to her lord, the bridle and the sword, the latter little used for such was his skill that few were foolhardy enough to test it. But now she must live without her lord and perhaps with another, Wyrd only knew. For holes could come quickly in the fabric of peace and often needed mending fast. Loose threads must be fastened before they were pulled and unravelled...

But the drummer and the horse had stopped. They had reached the graveside and there at her feet lay her lord in his cold, cold bed, shield and sword half covering his strong body, but helmet beside him, thank the gods, so she could see his sweet face. And now, young Manfried was tugging at her arm. Where should he put the oats he was carrying for the horse on its journey to the hall in the sky? Daughters too looked to her. Where should they put their gifts for their father? And now an elderman stepped forward and took the gifts, handed them to another, already in the grave, who put the roast meats in the coffin and the bucket outside it, near where the horse's head would rest.

Now he prepared to lower the coffin lid.

"Stop!" Maethilde felt her pulses racing. "A moment."

For her hands felt empty now. What could she give her lord to thank him for his gifts to her? What could she give him so that he would know she was his in the next life? Even as she thought these thoughts she was pulling the clasp from her left sleeve. Then, as the elderman led the horse to the other side of the grave, she knelt at the graveside, reached down and put it in her lover's hand.

A deer for my dear.

My heart for yours.

In death as in life.

There was no need for her to speak.

The drum began again.

Boom...

Boom...

Chapter 19

Hilde woke with the sound of a funeral drum in her ears. She'd been dreaming again, even though she no longer had the brooch. Friedman. Had he taken the brooch with him? Had he dreamed the same dream?

"Friendly fire ... Karl van Jennions ... family..."

As CNN boomed up from below she pictured the family round the fire at Pyghtle Cottage, but when she got downstairs she discovered that 'friendly fire' wasn't what she envisaged. Frank was muttering about an own goal. At first she didn't understand.

"Shot down by our own side." He shook his head in disbelief.

"Friendly fire is a mistake?"

He nodded. "Hideous, isn't it, specially when you think what friendly means. It's from the same root as

169

Freya, the Anglo-Saxon goddess of love. Sorry."

"Don't apologise." Hilde was surprised to find herself interested, and Frank's choice of words was spot on. Hideous was the word.

Before she set out for the dig she asked him to get her a book on human anatomy. She said – it was the truth but not the whole truth – that she wanted to learn the proper names of the bones. She also said she would start school next week.

"That's great, honey. I'll give the principal a call. What's today, Friday?" He looked so pleased she felt a twinge of guilt, but it was the only way. Whiston High, the highest building on the base, was the best place to stage her demo.

Later, as she walked past the school gate, she pictured the skeleton hanging from one of the top windows, with a huge banner drawing attention to it. Could she fix a banner up there without another pair of hands? Could she get someone else to help her?

"You coming in, miss?" A guard saw her looking at the building.

"No, not today." She said something about having to go to the dentist's and hurried on.

On BBC TV she'd seen British kids walking out of classes to protest against the war. Thousands were planning to go on the Hyde Park demo. In the papers commentators were saying that British youth was politicised at last. She'd had emails saying a big contingent from Crosby Upper was going to London. Sadie Marshall had started a Peace Weavers group. But nothing like that was happening here. As she passed the Junior High she heard a class chanting the oath of allegiance.

"I pledge allegiance to the flag of the United States of America and to the republic for which it stands, one nation under God, indivisible with liberty and justice for all."

Liberty and justice – was that really what Friedman's dad had died for?

As soon as she arrived on site Beth sent her to work in Trench 3 on her own. There was no one working in the warrior's trench, so all she had to do was keep her back to the CCTV camera. Quickly she labelled a plastic box LEFT LOWER LEG and put some stones in it to replace the leg she'd taken last night. There was no one in the finds shed when she stacked it with the others. Amy had gone to help to excavate a new trench that everyone was excited about – an archer's, which was even more rare than the warrior and his horse. A different weapon, so everyone was thrilled. Typical. As she walked to and fro she saw that several new trenches were being opened up. So everyone was busy and no one bothered her.

By eleven o'clock she'd hidden a thighbone in her backpack. She was about to go to the wooded area behind the finds shed – to look for something to put in the box as a substitute for it, when two oldish men came to look at the warrior's grave. She wasn't surprised to see new faces. A lot of new volunteers had turned up since the TV coverage, but she was surprised to see these two standing about doing nothing. Beth usually set people to work very quickly. Perhaps they'd just wandered in to have a look round. She was wondering whether to take her backpack with her or not, when one of them started to sound off.

"King Redwald, of Sutton Hoo, you know?" Very Bald had a pompous voice.

Not so Bald nodded.

"I think he gave this chap all that stuff they found with him, as a reward, for helping him in battle. This chap probably slaughtered hundreds. The Anglo-Saxons were a bloodthirsty lot."

"You're wrong actually." Hilde stood up, to Very Bald's surprise. He obviously hadn't noticed her before. "There's no evidence that the Anglo-Saxons massacred anyone."

"Oh," said Not so Bald. "Glad to hear it, my dear. But that's what we learned at school you see, that the Anglo-Saxons massacred the Celts unless they escaped to Scotland, Wales and Cornwall."

"Yes. So did I. It's what everyone learns about the Anglo-Saxons, but it's wrong. No one's found graves with the sort of injuries you get in massacres. They made raids, that's all, at first, because there was a shortage of land and food in Northern Europe, and then they stayed, but they were more like immigrants than invaders really."

"Immigrants, invaders – comes to the same thing in the end." Very Bald spluttered as he peered into the tall lady's grave. "My, she's a big girl! Why's she only got one leg? Was she one of those Amazon women? Bet she was a Women's Libber."

"Yes," said Hilde, taking a dislike to him. "She was, and she was a Peace Weaver."

Then Beth arrived with more boxes.

"Have you two come to help or admire the scenery?" she asked the men, and they scurried after her to the other side of the site.

By the end of the day Hilde had removed the whole of the right leg, and she'd thought about how she was going to join the skeleton together and display it. On the way home she stopped at the huge BX, which seemed to stock everything, and managed to find wool and a large-eyed needle. When she got home Frank gave her the book she'd asked for. It was a Body Atlas and just what she needed. She set to work straight after dinner. First she folded a single bed sheet in two lengthways. Then she bound the thighbone to it with wool. Then she added the lower leg bone. Before she went to bed she hid it in the suitcase she'd borrowed from Tom saying she needed somewhere to store her spare clothes. It looked quite good, but took much longer than she'd anticipated – and there were still more bones to sew on and even more to remove.

On Saturday morning she picked up that Frank was expecting her to start school on Monday and warned him that she wasn't.

He was annoyed. "But you said…"

"That I'd start next week, but I can't start Monday."

"Why not?"

"Because I'm in the middle of dismantling a skeleton, the Peace Weaver's skeleton. Beth asked me to and I need to give her notice."

The truth and yet not the truth.

"I'll go later in the week. Promise. Thursday, or Friday at the latest. I'll be finished then."

"Let's shake hands on that, Hilde. Let's not play games."

Friday 14th. Valentine's Day. She shook his hand. She had to go on Friday at the latest to take the skeleton to school.

Back in her room she went over her plan. If the guard at the school gate asked her to open the suitcase, she'd say the skeleton was for biology. Then she'd stay in school on Friday night, after ringing Frank to say that she'd been invited to a new friend's for a sleepover. Surely it wouldn't be that hard to hide in the school till everyone had left and then, on Saturday morning, when she'd tipped off the media on her mobile, suspend the skeleton and a banner from a window on one of the upper floors?

On Sunday she made the banner from another sheet. Bought black and red paint from the commissary.

WEAVE PEACE NOT WAR! It looked great. Monday and Tuesday went well. She was left to work on her own and by Tuesday night only the skull was left in the grave. She told Frank he could ring the school to say she was definitely starting Thursday. Only four days to go. Wednesday to remove the skull and fix it to the rest of the skeleton. Thursday to suss out the school. Friday to take it to school. Saturday – D-day, whether Myra Jennings and the Friends got their act together or not. They were cutting it a bit fine. She didn't even know if they'd got her ID card.

On Wednesday morning, February 12th, Frank handed her three envelopes.

"Early Valentines, honey?"

Grabbing them from his hand she shot upstairs.

Chapter 20

Two letters and a package – from America. She put it on one side, hardly daring to hope it was what she longed for it to be. Hoping the letter with writing she didn't recognise was the go-ahead for the demo on Saturday, she opened it first – and her ID card fell onto the floor.

Dear Hilde,
After much discussion and heart searching we have decided to postpone our demo on the base – indefinitely – because we are concentrating all our efforts on the Stop the War march on Feb 15th. We think it is important to make it the biggest demonstration that London has ever seen, so the government has to sit up and take notice. So I'm returning your ID card...

Hilde didn't read any more. Ruthie's letter was just as unhelpful.

Dear Hilde,
Sorry I haven't been in touch. I blame the technology! First my mobile didn't work in France. Then the family computer went berserk. Had to send it away for repair. Also had loads of work to catch up on. But the good news is that of COURSE you can come and stay with us! Mum and Dad both say you're very welcome. What about Half Term, Sat 22nd Feb – Sun March 2nd here? Is yours the same? But don't expect to play Happy Families. This one is split about Iraq. Like you I'm against the war full stop. It's STOOPID STOOPID STOOPID! Mum says she'll go along if the UN sanctions it, though she doesn't think they ought to. But Dad – DUH! – thinks Saddam Hussein will have to be removed by force. He says the UN have already passed loads of resolutions ordering him to get rid of his WMDs, but he hasn't, so war would be legal. Grandad – double DUH! – says Tony Blair knows what side his bread is buttered! Translation – attacking Iraq is wrong, but Britain has to go along with it, because USA are the Super Power, so we have to keep in with them.
BUT – some GOOD NEWS – Mum and I are both going on the march on 15th Feb. Are you? There's a busload going from here. Loads of people from school are coming, including Sadie Marshall who says your website is EXCELLENT!!! Can't wait to see it when computer comes back. She's started a Peace Weavers group and says she's

not the only one. You've started something BIG!
Loads of love,
Ruthie,
PS Let me know how many Valentines you get.
PPS WHAT was the 'stupid' thing you said you did?!!!
PPPS Tell me more about gorgeous Friedman. Are you
sure you're not projecting your own feelings onto me?
Can't see how you can't fancy him. Opposites attract,
remember!!!
PPPPS Send me ALL your phone numbers. Have lost.

How could Ruthie be so dumb? She hadn't asked for a
holiday. She wanted to live with the Curtises till Maeve
got back. Two dud letters.

With shaking hands she started to open the package
from America, pulled out a card and another bubble-
wrapped package. Yes! He had sent back the brooch. It
looked fine except for the missing stone. She opened the
card.

Dear Hilde,
I was on my way to give this back to you when I got the
news about my dad.
I saw the deer and now I'm giving it to you. Do whatever
you think is right.
Yours,
Friedman

P.S. I hope your mom got back safely.

178

Words were in her head. A deer for my dear. My heart for yours. Was that what he was saying? She wrote a reply before she had time to argue herself out of it:

Dear Friedman,
Thank you for returning the brooch. It means more than I can say, but perhaps you know that, as you say you saw the deer? I wish I could talk to you. I wish I could tell you how sorry I am that your dad has died – and mostly I wish I could think of words to stop you hurting. But I can't think of any. I can't think of anything comforting to say.
Yours, Hilde
PS I miss you.

Miss? Was that the word for what she felt? Had felt – or not felt – ever since he'd gone, because it was as if part of her had died. But his letter and the brooch revived painful feelings of hope and love. She added, 'I feel that part of me has died,' then determined to do what she could to stop other dads getting killed, she set off for the site, swept along by a flood of emotion. It was as if a dam had burst. A sudden shower of rain seemed to suit her mood. Reaching the Post Office, she dropped her reply into the mailbox, then ran the rest of the way.

There was only the skull to remove from the trench now. If she worked fast she could get it out by lunchtime. Then she'd make her excuses, nip back to Frank's and attach it to the rest of the skeleton. Then she'd ring the local papers to tip them off that there was going to be a photo opportunity on the base on Saturday morning.

She arrived at the site. At first it seemed deserted. Then she saw Beth, Sid and Amy and Very Bald, the new volunteer she disliked, huddled in the doorway of the finds shed. Oddly, she didn't suspect that anything was wrong. She thought they were sheltering from the rain. Then she noticed the rain had stopped and Beth was beckoning her over.

She looked worried and sympathetic.

"I don't know how to tell you this, Hilde. Something weird has happened… All your hard work…" She shook her head as if she couldn't believe what she was saying. 'The fact is, Hilde, someone's stolen your Peace Weaver's skeleton."

Hilde noticed that Very Bald didn't look so sympathetic. In fact he didn't look sympathetic at all. He was looking straight at her.

Beth said, "Have you two met? David, Mr Jackson, is a volunteer and, fortunately for us, a police officer. He says it shouldn't be hard to find the thief and hopefully get the skeleton back."

Sid said, "Mebbe it's a student stunt."

Beth shook her head. "All the students have gone back to uni."

"But there's no sign of a break-in," said Very Bald, "so it's got to be an inside job. Someone who works on site must have done it. If no one owns up sharpish we'll get there by a process of elimination. For a start we can examine the empty containers for fingerprints."

"There'll be Hilde's of course," said Beth. "And Amy's perhaps."

"Naturally," said Very Bald. "The question is – will there be anyone else's?"

All the time he spoke he never took his eyes off Hilde.

Chapter 21

Hilde started to feel sick. Did anyone else suspect her? Had Very Bald voiced his very obvious suspicions before she arrived?

Amy was wringing her hands. "This puts me in a difficult position. The finds are in my care when they're on site. Should I have kept the door locked? Frisked everyone as they came in and out?"

Beth said, "No, Amy. That would make for an impossible working atmosphere. We have to trust people. In fact I'm going to call a meeting and ask everyone straight out if they've taken it for any reason."

Other people were arriving on site. Beth told Sid to ask them all to come to the office, straightaway. "They'll have to gather outside because there isn't enough room in. I just hope the rain holds off."

As Sid and then Beth went off, Amy turned to Hilde.

"I came in this morning to start cataloguing the skeleton in Trench 3. I opened a box you'd marked Left Hand and found stones in it. It's so odd. There were sticks and stones in some boxes and not others. Why would a thief go to all that trouble, but only some of the time?"

Hilde shrugged. She didn't say because I was running out of time and couldn't always find any suitable sticks and stones.

"There's another odd thing," Amy went on. "They haven't taken the skull. It's still in the trench. Why would they leave that?"

"Why indeed?" Very Bald stayed close, Hilde noticed, when the three of them walked to the office, to join the workers gathered round the steps.

Soon Beth came out and explained why she'd called the meeting.

"First of all I'd like to ask if anyone has taken the skeleton as a joke. If anyone has, I'm afraid it will mean instant dismissal, but if it's returned now unharmed, then charges won't be made. But this is your last chance to take advantage of that amnesty, so please, if you have taken it, for any reason, say so now, before we involve the police."

No one spoke.

Hilde could feel her heart beating.

"Anyone?" Beth looked from face to face.

Hilde felt hers reddening, but if she confessed now it would be a complete waste. She'd just got to keep quiet, deny everything, for two more days.

"Please," appealed Beth, "if you know anything at all about this, speak up now and save us a lot of trouble. Wasting police time would be another serious offence."

Silence.

"Very serious," said Very Bald.

"Well then, I trust you'll all co-operate with the police when they arrive. Your fingerprints will probably be taken. Please will no one leave the site till the investigation has taken place?" Then Beth dismissed the meeting, apologising again for having to say what she did.

Everyone – except Very Bald and Beth – went back to the jobs they'd been doing. As Hilde went back to hers she heard Very Bald suggest that he contact colleagues at the police station and arrange for the fingerprinting. It would be quicker that way, he said. They might take ages to come otherwise, if they came at all. The super might not consider it a priority.

Feeling even sicker Hilde watched him drive off site a few minutes later.

She carried on carefully removing the soil round the back of the skull, while wondering what to do. It was going to be impossible to get the skull off site now. Everyone was watching everyone else. If she got caught trying it would stymie everything. She'd have to display a headless skeleton or give up.

"What'll I do, Maethilde? What'll I do?"

Crouched in the bottom of the trench, she felt like a fox at bay. The hounds were getting closer by the minute. They were going to get her. She might as well give up. Then, as she was putting on white gloves to lift the skull out, she saw a tiny red grain of something by the skeleton's left ear. Could it be...? She picked it up – and her racing heart skipped a beat as it showed up clearly against the white of her gloved hand. It wasn't sparkling, the day was too dull for that, but it was the stone, a garnet. It seemed like an omen. Don't give up. She picked it up, wrapped it in a tissue and put it in her pocket with the brooch.

Very Bald was soon back, in uniform now and in a police car. He and two other officers got out, a man and woman, and headed for the office. Then, as Hilde was putting the skull in a box lined with acid free paper, Beth came over to Trench 3.

"Sorry to stop you getting on, but I'm afraid I must ask you to come to the finds shed and identify the boxes you put there – and have your fingerprints taken."

Why was she so apologetic, Hilde wondered, as she covered the skull with the lid. Because she felt sorry for her? Or was she being nice to encourage her to confess?

"You were the last person to see the boxes full," Beth went on. "That's why the police have got to speak to you. Except the thief of course," she added quickly.

Before she set off after her Hilde picked up the box containing the skull.

Amy was just inside the finds shed pressing her fingers on an inky pad. It looked strangely low tech and unreal, as if she was in an old-fashioned detective serial.

Beth introduced Hilde to the WPC taking the prints.

"This is Hilde Browne, one of my best volunteers."

Feeling a twinge of guilt Hilde noticed that Very Bald wasn't in the shed. A young male PC was sprinkling black dust on one of the plastic boxes, saying finger-printing was a routine measure that might help a lot.

"Once we've identified and eliminated everyone who's legitimately handled the boxes we'll know if anyone else has. We can check them all quickly back at the station."

"But wouldn't a thief have worn gloves?" asked Beth. "And we wear gloves when handling finds."

Hilde was still wearing hers, and was hoping she always had when handling the boxes when Very Bald came in.

"Now let's go over this again," he barked. "You say that Hilde here was responsible for uncovering the skeleton and bringing the parts here? How do you know she brought them here? What checks were there?"

"None," said Amy. "As I said, we trust people."

Very Bald raised bushy eyebrows.

Hilde felt pressure mounting.

She put down the boxed skull. She'd have to display a headless skeleton. Now she could feel her heart thudding.

"Well?" said Very Bald. He'd asked her something but she hadn't heard.

"I said – describe to us exactly what happened when

you last came to this room, when you were standing at this table."

The hound was baring its teeth.

Her insides were turning to liquid.

"I'll say it again," said Very Bald as the door opened.

"Oh no!" said Beth. "Not them. Not now. Who told them?"

"Pam Powling, BBC TV East," said a reporter Hilde recognised. "We've heard there's been a robbery." Behind her was a man with a video camera on his shoulder.

Very Bald tugged his lapels, obviously relishing his moment of fame. "I'm warning you, Hilde Browne, you do not have to say anything, but it may harm your defence if you do not mention when questioned, something you later rely on in court. Anything you do say may be used in evidence. Now, did you knowingly, over a period of days, steal a skeleton from this site?"

The moment had come. Hilde knew she must speak, now, while the cameras were rolling. But she'd left the speech she'd written for Saturday in her bedroom. Would the words come out right, or at all? Word weave. Peace weave. Now.

Deep breath. "Yes, I Hilde Webster stole the skeleton of Maethilde the Peace Weaver!" As she spoke she lifted the skull out of the box and held it in front of the camera. "I enrolled a Peace Weaver from the past to help me peace weave for the future, because…because…" Everyone was staring at her – or maybe at the skull.

Keep going.

"...because, well, I had to do something. Peace weaving, it's about making connections, looking for solutions, talking – which I'm not exactly brilliant at. But I've been trying to get better because I'm fed up with people fighting, not working things out, not talking, not discussing – internationally – or in families." But best not go there. "Conflict hurts – that's so obvious it shouldn't need saying, but it does, hurt I mean, even when it's just words, and people in the crossfire get hurt too. But weapons hurt fatally, and arguments can be used to solve conflict..."

At last some of her written speech came back to her.

"People have known for hundreds of years that you've got to create peace, resolve conflicts with words and actions. In Maethilde's day – that's whose skull this is – it was a woman's main role, her job, and it had high status. Men admired women's peace-weaving skills and consulted them about how to do it. But for some reason that hasn't gone into most history books and today, incredibly, we still see war as a solution to conflict, even when our weapons are a thousand times more destructive than in those days. So things are worse now, because the military drop bombs on people they can't even see, so they don't really know what they're doing.

"I'm protesting against the war with Iraq, but it's not just a protest against that war or any war. I'm campaigning for peaceful solutions, for using the United Nations, which is a brilliant peace-weaving network actually, for letting weapons inspectors carry on looking for Weapons of Mass Destruction, for disarming Iraq if they find any. Dropping bombs on Iraqi people – to get rid of one man – it's stupid. It's cruel. It's unfair. It'll do more harm than good. So that's why I'm urging people to become Peace Weavers and Stop the War!"

It wasn't oratory, but she'd said, at last, what she wanted to say. She added, "If you want to know more go to *www.peaceweavers.com.*"

Pam Powling beamed. "A triumph!"

But that wasn't the word for the feeling inside Hilde as Very Bald snapped shut his notebook and gripped her arm. He said, "Come this way, please, young lady," and led her outside.

Chapter 22

Very Bald took her to the office, where Sid rang Frank, though Hilde said it was nothing to do with him.

"Didn't you notice that I used my mother's surname?"

Beth glared at her. "Sounds to me as if it's got quite a bit to do with Frank, but where's the skeleton, Hilde?" She was shaking with anger. " What have you done with it?"

"I haven't hurt it."

"Dr Stansfield asked where not how it was." Very Bald stood with his back to the door as if he thought Hilde might make a run for it.

She felt like kicking him – that's why peace weaving was so hard – but sat down to show she wasn't going anywhere. "I had a reason."

"Obviously." Beth said something to Very Bald and he

left, and Hilde remembered the brooch and the garnet.

"You'd better have these too. Be careful with the tissue, there's something tiny inside." She emptied her pockets onto the desk in front of her, and as she unwrapped the packages Beth gasped. But Hilde felt drained of emotion, and knew her deadpan voice must sound uncaring as she tried to explain.

"I found them, it – the garnet is part of the brooch – in the Peace Weaver's grave on my first day here. The brooch is the third part of the sleeve clasp and it's identical to the one in the warrior's grave, and once I had it, I started to have vivid dreams about her – and him – and somehow I never managed to give it back, till today."

Beth was gazing at the brooch on the desk.

"He, her husband, the warrior," Hilde went on, "he died of marsh fever by the way, which broke her heart, but she forced herself to carry on with the work they were doing together."

"Which was?" said Sid, as Beth shook her head.

"Peace weaving."

"Women's work?" said Sid.

"Yes, but they worked together. They had to because revenge feuds were such a huge problem at the time. Most people felt they lost face by coming to terms, and if they or their family was hurt, they wanted to hurt back. There was a system to try and stop it..."

"Yes yes, the manprice, we do know this, Hilde. It's in books." Beth sounded exasperated, but Sid said,

"Go on, 'ilde. You say the couple we've found were peace makers?"

"Peace Weavers, yes. His sword was a reward from the king for keeping the peace. He could fight, and that reputation helped him keep the peace, but mostly he liked making things. He made the sleeve clasps."

Beth picked up the brooch when she saw Hilde glance at it.

Sid said, "Carry on, 'ilde."

"The clasps were a strong link between them. They, Maethilde and Manfried, were about to fight each other once, but then he saw she was wearing the clasps and stopped. It was a turning point. Killing his stepbrother, to save Maethilde's life, was another, for both of them. They both watched the young man dying on the sand in front of them, and it strengthened their resolve to be Peace Weavers."

"It's good stuff," said Sid, glancing at Beth who still looked angry. "And you say you dreamed it all up?"

But before Hilde could answer Frank walked in looking ashen. "Honey, what's up?" In seconds he was beside her. "I just got this message to come here. I thought...accident...or worse. Thank God..." He scrutinised Hilde as if checking for injury, then turned angrily to the others. "Couldn't you have at least told me she was safe?"

Beth said, "Sorry, Frank. She's been stealing, but says it's nothing to do with you."

"I'm her dad, Beth. Hilde and I are in this together."

In the afternoon she was allowed to go home with him after making statements and promising not to abscond. Frank had to sign a declaration, a bit like bail, and so did she. Then Beth came with them to collect the skeleton. She was shocked when she saw it bound to the sheet.

"This is vandalism, Hilde. I thought you cared about archaeology and had a flair for it. That's why I took a chance on you. You betrayed my trust – and Frank's."

As she picked up the suitcase she said. "I hope we don't both lose our jobs because of this."

It was a mess. No one seemed to know what would happen next, though a court case seemed inevitable at some time in the future. When Frank went out to buy something for tea Tom launched an attack. "How could you? How could you do it to Frank when he's been so decent?"

"Because there are bigger things at stake." She tried to explain, but Tom said he'd heard it all before from Maeve.

"And everyone here's going to know that I'm your brother."

"Sorry – about that. You can disown me if you like."

"And you say you might be on TV?" He winced at the thought of it.

She was on TV, on the BBC 6 o'clock news. The three of them watched it while eating pizza on their knees in the lounge, Tom on the end of the sofa, near the door as if ready for a quick getaway. The national news was mostly about troops going out to Iraq and preparations for the Stop the War demo in Hyde Park. It ended without a mention of Hilde. But then the local news started and Hilde's protest was the first item.

"Today, at Whiston USAF Base, a defiant young woman who can't be named for legal reasons has protested against military action in Iraq,' said Pam Powling. Then Hilde's fuzzed out face appeared, and her distorted voice. 'I...funny noise...stole the skeleton of Maethilde the Peace Weaver. I enrolled a Peace Weaver from the past to help me peace weave for the future, because..."

Tom watched from behind his hands, as if it were a horror movie.

Hilde couldn't help feeling thrilled. Her speech didn't sound too bad, and they broadcast all of it. It was publicity for the cause – that was the main thing.

Afterwards, the reporter said the young woman had planned an even more spectacular demonstration involving the skeleton, but this had been foiled when a police officer working on site as a volunteer became suspicious. Film taken earlier came on – of the Peace Weaver still in her grave. The reporter added, "Stealing from an archaeological site can carry a six months' jail sentence, or a hefty fine, but the young woman is legally a minor and the County Archaeologist is considering what action to take."

Beth appeared briefly to confirm this, but handed over to Meri when asked what the young woman meant by Peace Weaving.

"In Anglo-Saxon times it was a woman's main role..." As Meri began Tom left the room.

It was excellent publicity, especially as the newsreader linked Hilde's protest with Saturday's peace march, and local interest in it. Hundreds of people were heading for London, twenty coaches full, and extra trains were being laid on.

"I wish..." said Hilde, when her beautiful pink mobile rang. It was Ruthie – at last!

The next hour was a frenzied bout of phone calls. Hilde talked to Ruthie. "Please, please, please can I come and stay with you?" Ruthie talked to her mum. Hilde talked to Frank. Frank talked to Ruthie's mum. Frank talked to Beth and the police and the deputy commander of the base to see if Hilde was allowed to leave.

"Would that count as "absconding"?" she heard him say, and when he came back from the phone, he said everyone he'd asked said they'd be heartily relieved if she left the base and never came back.

"And you?"

He didn't answer. She wasn't sure if he'd heard or not, and for a moment she felt rejected, but only a moment as the good news dawned. She could go to Ruthie's! She might even be able to go on the march!

Frank drove her to Ruthie's next day. They set off after breakfast for the long drive to Merseyside. For once she was glad of his classical music, which filled the silence between them. She enjoyed it in fact and wondered if she'd been brainwashed by hearing so much. One tape had a surging rhythm as if striving towards some ecstatic climax, and that's what she felt – as if she was heading for victory, the march on Saturday!

But between tapes she waited for Frank to say something. He must be angry, must be; his job and house were at risk. She'd caused him a lot of trouble. That was one of the things she regretted. When they stopped at a pub for a meal, shortly before they got to Crosby, she couldn't stand the silence any longer. It was worse than rowing. She had to say something, had to make him say something. When they were sitting opposite each other at a small pub table she confronted him.

"Just say it, please, that you're angry."

He look puzzled.

"About your job and everything?"

"But I'm not."

"What then? I want to know how you feel for heaven's sake."

"Feel?" He seemed surprised. "Oh. Well. To be honest, I am a bit relieved to get you off the base for a bit, and yes, I have felt angry, but…" He shrugged. "All this, everything that's happened, may be a good thing. I like to think I've been doing my bit on base. All librarians are subversives. We peddle ideas. But, if I've

196

gotta go, well, I never did intend staying so long, and I can probably get another job off base now. And whatever happens, Hilde" – he looked at her earnestly, too earnestly – "I'd like you to know, I have no regrets. I'm glad I've got to know you better. I love and admire you and I'm sorry for the hurt I've caused in your life."

Gulp.

When they got back in the car he said there was a little present for her in the glove compartment. It was a book with an elephant on the cover.

"British author, American setting, gutsy hero and heroine. I think you'll like it. I didn't get Babar, because well, we can't go back, can we, Hilde, but maybe we can go forward?"

Double gulp. The title blurred as he started the car. She thought it was called *The Great Elephant Chase*, and if he hadn't been driving she'd have hugged him.

Soon afterwards they arrived at Ruthie's house on the corner of Cambridge Road, and there was Ruthie, with her hair cut so short, Hilde nearly didn't recognise her, rushing out of the door, shrieking welcomes. Frank came in for a coffee – and, Hilde thought, to check that the Curtises were OK people – but he didn't stay long. She gave him a big hug when they said goodbye.

"Keep in touch, honey. Whoops."

She laughed and waved her little mobile. "Of course. I'll ring and text you."

Early on Saturday morning, squashed between Ruthie

and her mum, she set off for London. It was exhilarating from the moment she stepped onto the coach – to loud hurrahs from a gang from school all wearing Peace Weavers sweatshirts! The logo she'd designed of a multi-coloured woven globe looked great. Several teachers welcomed her too. As Mrs Milligan waddled down the gangway she said, "Thought you lot slept through my Citizenship lessons," but she looked thrilled. Excitement mounted as the convoy moved through the sleepy Merseyside streets heading for the M6. Soon people began to sing campaigning favourites like 'We shall overcome' and 'Give peace a chance' and as traffic built up it seemed as if the whole world was heading for London. Hilde wished her mum were there too.

By mid morning when they reached the outskirts the streets were full of people, some of them already holding their banners high. STOP THE WAR, NOT IN OUR NAME, DON'T ATTACK IRAQ and NO BLOOD FOR OIL. The Crosby crowd streamed out of the coach into a sea of bodies swirling round the streets. Hilde soon spotted a forest of hands surrounding a HANDS UP FOR PEACE banner. With Ruthie's help she unfurled her own WEAVE PEACE NOT WAR banner and hoisted it high! Soon other Peace Weaver groups joined them.

Hilde had been on demos before with Maeve. Often they'd been pathetically small and it had been hard not to feel embarrassed standing in a shopping centre being stared at. She'd sometimes wondered what the point was when she was sitting outside a nuclear base in the wilds of Scotland, and hardly anyone noticed. Maeve was never embarrassed. She said they were voices crying in the wilderness and their day would come – and now it seemed it had. Hilde felt part of something huge. As the crowd surged down Park Lane towards Hyde Park, she felt as if her feet were above the ground; as if she was part of a sea of bodies, carried along on a tide of enthusiasm.

It was the biggest demonstration the capital had ever seen, and huge screens in the park showed the same thing happening all over the world! Millions and millions of people were marching for peace. They weren't just a noisy minority, though they were noisy. Bands played. Crowds chanted. And opinion polls showed that most people were against the war.

As Hilde climbed onto the coach at the end of the day, she felt buoyed with confidence. For the first time ever a demo had felt right and effective. It would achieve something. As Ruthie flopped down beside her on the back seat she said, "The government can't ignore us now."

But the government did. The war began on Thursday March 20th. Hilde felt as if the tide had turned and crashed her against the rocks.

Chapter 23

"Mum!"

"Hilde, wake up! What is it?" Ruthie was by her side, rubbing her frozen hands, as she crouched under the bedclothes.

She'd been dreaming of Maeve.

Earlier that night, huddled on Ruthie's bed, they'd watched the start of the war, seen bombs exploding over Baghdad, heard commentators making it sound like a firework display or a computer game called Shock and Awe! A hit! The bombers had got a hit! A government building that Saddam used! A restaurant he was eating in! They'd scored! Got Saddam Hussein in the first hour of bombing!

It was good at least to have Ruthie's arm round her as she wondered where her mum was. Some members of the Human Shield had left Baghdad a couple of days earlier – they'd seen that on the TV too – but British Nurse Mother of Two wasn't among them. Maeve had stayed to help. That was the last Hilde had heard of her.

Next day at school arguments raged between the Pro- and Anti-war parties, but Hilde felt too depressed to join in. She'd taken part in heated discussions ever since she'd gone back to school, but now she couldn't summon the energy. The bombing went on. Saddam's body hadn't been found. One week, two weeks, three passed and she tried not to think about what was happening where the bombs fell. She felt as if she'd joined the Don't Cares who yawned as they passed the Pros and Antis arguing in classroom or corridor. There were a lot of Don't Cares. Crosby Upper wasn't quite the hotbed of revolution she'd pictured when she was stuck on Whiston Base. There was anti-war feeling, about a third of the school she guessed, but just as many war enthusiasts, led by Beckham look-alike James O'Connor. His brother was in the army and he was in the school's Air Training Corps, who marched round the playground on Wednesday afternoons.

It was Wednesday April 9th when James turned up in the dinner hall, wearing camouflage gear, and obviously looking for someone. Hilde was in the queue with Ruthie and Sadie when she saw him approaching.

"Ah there you are!" He grabbed Sadie's arm. "Follow me, you peaceniks. Want to show you something."

"Where are we going?" Sadie didn't shrug him off, Hilde noticed, as she and Ruthie trogged along behind.

"To the TV in the resources room."

Word had obviously gone round that something was happening there, because there were others heading that way and the resources room was full when they arrived.

"Look at that!" James, exultant, pointed over people's heads at the TV screen, and they saw a statue of Saddam Hussein falling from a pedestal.

"All over in three weeks," said James when the cheering on the screen and in the resources room died down. "Don't you feel daft?"

"Don't you?" said Ruthie, holding up a photo of a boy whose arms had been shot off by a cluster bomb. "Not over in three weeks for him."

"One boy," said James. "Saddam killed thousands. Mass graves exposed. Torture chambers revealed. What more do you want?"

"WMDs found, our reason for invading, sorry, liberating Iraq?"

"You wait," said James.

"We will," said Ruthie.

But Sadie said she was reconsidering. If she saw a distinct improvement in the lives of the Iraqi people, she'd have to conclude that the invasion had been worth it.

Ruthie tutted. "You mean you fancy James?"

The arguments went on till Friday when school broke up for the Easter holiday.

During the holiday Hilde had even more time to think. Did the end justify the means? Had it been a 'good war' ending a 'bad peace'? The mass graves and torture chambers were proof of Saddam Hussein's evil regime. What was Friedman thinking, she wondered, as she had a message about her mum, from one of the returning Human Shield members. Maeve was OK. Friedman wouldn't be getting a cheery message about his dad. He was in her thoughts more and more as the war ended officially, a couple of days later – after twenty-seven days – but the killing went on. Soldiers not much older than him were returning to the UK and the USA in body bags. There was more opposition to the liberating forces than anticipated. Commentators talked of the need for a continuing military presence in Iraq. Did Friedman still want to follow in his father's footsteps? If so he could be heading for Iraq in a couple of years.

He hadn't answered her letter. She checked with Frank who she phoned quite often. He said there was no post for her at all. If any did arrive he'd forward it rightaway. He was expecting her summons, he said, but that hadn't arrived either. She'd pushed that to the back of her mind, hoped that maybe charges would be dropped. Frank said he didn't think they would be, and that he thought Hilde would be fined, might even get probation. He'd spoken to Beth who was under a lot of pressure to go ahead with a court case. Next day Hilde rang several stores about Saturday jobs in case she had a fine to pay.

Ruthie soon spotted that there were things on her mind. Hilde told her about the possible trial, but not about her letter to Friedman, and how silly she now felt for sending it. But therapist Ruthie prised the whole story from her, on Easter Sunday morning as they ate their way through a pile of Easter eggs.

"What's up, Hild? Chocolate's supposed to have a cheering effect on the brain. I know there's something else. Tell. You'll feel better for it."

She did a bit, but was worried now, that she'd been wrong about the war.

"You're kidding?" Ruthie had no doubts at all. "How can you be worried about lover boy coming back in a body bag and think war may be right? You – we – were – are right to be anti-war. It's chaos in Baghdad now with armed criminals and terrorists roaming the streets – Al Qaida's in the country though they weren't before – so that aid agencies are too scared to move in. Meanwhile Iraqi people are still without water or electricity or medical supplies. It's the same old story. Governments are good at bombing people, crap at peace weaving. Our campaign was and is about changing that."

TV and newspapers confirmed what Ruthie said and Hilde began to worry about Maeve again. She hadn't heard from her lately. Was she still OK?

Yes! But Hilde didn't know that till a fortnight later when she woke up to a fanfare of hoots. Peering out of the window, she saw her mother's rainbow striped

Volvo parked on a yellow line outside the Curtises' house. Then she saw Maeve, leaner and browner, jumping out, and waving when she saw Hilde.

"You can't go out like that," spluttered Mrs Curtis as Hilde whooshed past her on the stairs, propelled by relief and joy. Only when she was hugging and being hugged by Maeve, did she truly realise how desperately worried she had been and how much she'd missed her. But here she was safe and well and laughing and crying. Both of them were bawling happily. That was what was so wonderful about Maeve. She didn't bother about petty things like crying in public or being outside in your nightie, and she was fun. She did what she did because she wanted to – and she wanted to put the world to rights. If the spirit moves you, do it! That was her motto. If it doesn't, don't.

But Mrs Curtis was frosty when Maeve reached the doorstep. Hilde had overheard her once asking Mr Curtis what people like Maeve would do, if there weren't people like them to pick up the pieces? But Maeve didn't seem to notice the frostiness. She hugged Mrs Curtis too, then dived back into the car and came out with a big jar of raspberry jam.

"It's from Bulgaria. A little thank you for having Hilde. I thought she was at her father's. Went there first you know. US guards wouldn't even let me on the base. Frank had to come to the gates to meet me."

Mrs Curtis looked mystified. Hilde laughed at the thought of Maeve's rainbow painted car on base, till suddenly, she thought of Friedman, longing for his dad to come back. No ecstatic reunion for him.

Oddly it was awkward when she and Maeve were together again, heading for the campsite in Blundell-sands. It was a lovely May morning, and it was great not to have to feel like a picked-up piece, but sometimes hard to respond to Maeve who expected her to agree with everything she said. "Tom didn't want to come back," she said, sounding surprised and hurt. "He didn't even come with Frank to see me."

"He likes living on base."

"And you didn't? That figures." Maeve cheered up. "Tell me, tell me everything, Hilde."

"Later. Frank's OK you know."

"Ah! You fell for his charms! Don't tell me, Hilde – like I did once. I loved him once, you know, till he sold out."

"I don't think he did sell out."

"He went to live on an American base!"

"But he didn't sell out. And he didn't walk out, not in the way you let me think." As she spoke, Hilde felt something mesh inside her – the war inside her at least was over.

Silence. Maeve didn't get it.

Hilde mentioned the dig and her dreams, and tried to explain about peace weaving.

"It's not just about international relations. It's also about family and friendship too."

"Of course it is."

"And marriage."

"Are you getting at me, Hild?"

"I just think it's more complicated than you think. It's an intricate fabric, woven thread by thread, full of bright colours, but also black and white and quite a lot of grey."

"Well, I never did like grey," Maeve laughed as she turned the Volvo into the campsite and drove up to their rainbow-striped caravan. "Let's get the kettle on, then you can tell me about this court case that's coming up."

"It might not happen."

"Bet it does."

Maeve was right. Three weeks later, on a Friday morning, just as Hilde was setting off for school, her summons arrived in the post. It said she had to appear in Bury St Edmunds' Magistrates Court in two weeks' time. Suddenly it felt scary and too close, though Frank had warned her it was on its way and said he would, of course, go with her. He'd also said he'd appointed a solicitor to defend her in court.

Maeve said, "Welcome it as an opportunity, Hild. And come straight home tonight. We'd better start thinking about what we're going to say at your trial."

"We? It's my trial!"

It was good though, to have her to talk it over with. She had a lot of experience. Like Frank, she thought there would be a fine, so Hilde was glad she'd been working at TJ Hughes for the last few Saturdays. She just hoped it wouldn't be a massive fine. She wanted to pay it herself, and be as independent as possible.

But on the day of the trial, she had to admit, there was something nice about walking into the imposing Victorian building, flanked by her mum and dad, though she'd sworn Maeve to silence. As they climbed the steps to the entrance, a contingent of Friends appeared from the churchyard next door. They waved banners and cheered, but Hilde noted the police officers by the doors, and that the basement windows were barred as if there were cells below. She started to worry about what might happen to her if the magistrates weren't sympathetic. It felt scary, and would have been scarier without Frank and Maeve.

In a room next to the courtroom she met the solicitor who was defending her. Ms Hill was grey haired to Hilde's surprise. She'd sounded younger on the phone when she'd rung to ask lots of questions – about Hilde's early life as well as her time on base. Now she was brisk as she ushered them into the courtroom, which looked much like Hilde had expected from TV programmes.

The magistrates, two men and a woman, didn't wear wigs and gowns, but they looked stern as they took their places on the bench. Beth, sitting opposite Hilde, on the prosecution side, looked even sterner, though Frank had said she felt bad about bringing the matter to court. But when Beth, as Dr Stansfield, was called to the stand and started to describe the offences, Hilde began to think she might get sent to a young offender institute. Her crimes seemed so bad she almost believed she deserved to go to one. Later, PC Jackson, Very Bald, gave evidence and he sounded as if he'd like to send her to one.

But Hilde did get a chance to tell her side of things, and she tried to tell it exactly as she remembered. The prosecuting solicitor, a young man, cross-examined her.

"But you *deliberately* took the skeleton?"

"Yes."

"So you *weren't* sorry for your previous theft of a gold brooch."

"I was in a way."

"You were sorry *in a way*." He sat down without giving her a chance to try and explain.

Ms Hill tried to be helpful. "Hilde, tell the court in what way you're sorry."

"I'm sorry if I did any damage to either the brooch or the skeleton of the Peace Weaver. I'm sorry I've got myself a bad reputation. I don't want to make excuses, but I've never stolen anything before. I took the skeleton to make a protest against the war, and I'm glad I did, make the protest I mean, but I still don't know why I took the brooch. All I can say is that I never intended to keep it and I was really pleased and relieved to give it back."

It was wonderful seeing the brooch, Exhibit A, once again, when a court official held it out before her, so she could identify it. It shone under the lights of the court.

"You say you have never stolen anything before?" said the chief magistrate.

"Never."

"And can you promise never to do so again?"

"Yes. I can."

Hilde sat down and soon afterwards Ms Hill summed up the case for the defence. She went on and on about the stress suffered by her client. Sometimes Hilde found it hard to recognise the poor creature she described, deserted by her mother, forced to live in an alien environment with a father she didn't know. But it seemed to weigh heavily with the magistrates – or maybe the brooch worked its magic – for after some deliberation with his colleagues, the chief magistrate reprimanded Hilde severely for stealing, but then bound her over to keep the peace! No problem!

Maeve was amazed at the result, but she was even more amazed, a week later, when Hilde said she wanted to go to Karl van Jennions' Memorial Service.

"Why, Hilde? It'll be jingoistic claptrap."

"I know but I want to go."

The invitation, sent on by Frank, from Pyghtle Cottage, made her catch her breath.

Ruthie wasn't amazed. At school she said what she'd said many times before over the previous weeks.

"You've got the hots for Friedman, Hilde – and he for you!"

"He thinks I'm a thief."

Ruthie scoffed.

"I stole a skeleton and a valuable antique brooch."

"And why?"

Hilde still couldn"t answer that question, not about the brooch anyway.

"Your sub-conscious, Hild..."

"Bollocks, Ruthie."

"Exactly. Your language is very revealing. Stealing can be a cry from the heart." She demanded to see the letter from Marty that came with the invitation. It said that the service was going to be a celebration of Karl's life and she wanted people to dress cheerfully.

"Right, so what are you going to wear?"

Ruthie had another bit of news. She'd checked the Peace Weavers' website, where an impassioned debate was going on as to the nature of Peace Weaving. Ruthie was fully engaged in the debate, but something else had excited her.

"A certain Friedman van Jennions has signed your petition. Is that an amazing coincidence or what?'

Hilde checked it later and began to feel hopeful.

Chapter 24

Frank met her at Bury St Edmunds station. It was the first time she'd seen him since the trial.

"You look nice," Frank said hugging her.

"So do you." It was very good to see him.

He laughed. "Tom took me shopping to the summer sales. The flowery shirt's a Paul Smith."

"Mine's a Ruthie Curtis." It was blue silk and looked like a dress on Ruthie. "But the combats are my own."

He laughed. "You and your combats. What's a peace weaver doing in combats? That blue suits you," he added. It was the blue of the flax in the fields they were passing. She'd tied her hair back with a scarf the same colour.

For a few miles they did the How's Maeve? How's Tom? Lovely weather routine as the flat fenland flew past. Then suddenly it seemed they were in a line of vehicles waiting at the base gates – and they glanced at each other with a sense of Been Here Before. The summer sky was blue and white as it had been that January day when she'd arrived – till the jets scrawled all over it – but there were no jets today. The queue of cars was longer though. Frank inched the car forward as the barrier ahead rose and the military descended on another vehicle.

"Sorry about this. In…"

"…creased alert. I know." There had been a terrorist attack the day before, the third on American targets since the war on Iraq. Thirty killed. Two hundred injured. She'd read the papers on the way up.

"So much for the war making the world a safer place." Frank shook his head. "Jury's still out I guess, but there's one thing we can be sure of, Hilde, the truth will out, in the US anyway. We'll know who lied, if anyone did."

"Why not here?"

"Well, it'll get here, if we find anything, but the Brits aren't so hot on freedom of information. Not sure why. Maybe there's a bit of keeping the lower orders in their place?"

"Pass." Hilde looked at her watch. 2 o'clock.

The service was at 3 and they had to get Tom first. Frank picked up a CD and the name Brunnhilde caught her eye. There she was galloping into the middle of a bonfire.

213

"Excuse me." The old anger was rising. "I've been meaning to ask, why did you name me after that mad woman?"

"Brunnhilde? Mad? Don't you know the story?"

She shook her head as he moved the car forward.

"Well Brunnhilde was a goddess, one of the Valkyrie who scooped the dead from battlefields, but she chose to be human, sacrificed her own immortality so she could love another human being. Is that mad?"

She shook her head again.

"I think she was magnificent. Listen."

Then the car filled with music so beautiful she wanted to cry.

*

Tom was getting worried by the time they picked him up. He was waiting on the doorstep and greeted Hilde warily as he dived into the back of the car. "Hope you're not going to make a show of yourself."

They reached the chapel in time, just. The paved area round it was empty, except for piles of flowers, and armed personnel by the doors. Inside was packed, mostly with uniformed military and as they found standing space at the back an organ began to play 'I Vow to thee my Country'. The rest of the congregation got to their feet. Then Marty, wearing an orange trouser suit, was walking past them up the aisle, head held high, swinging her arms as if she was in the military, flanked by two upright elderly women. And then came Friedman holding the hands of his sisters – and Hilde's heart

214

leaped. She felt it thumping inside her ribcage so hard that it hurt and it kept on hurting throughout the service as she watched the back of his head and shoulders. He was on the front row, with his arms round his sisters who snuggled into him as the service went on and on and on. She guessed Olivia was crying, because at one point he leaned towards her as if he were wiping her eyes. But what was he thinking, what was he feeling she wondered, as the chaplain and other people praised his dad and his country, and said it was sad but wonderful that the one had sacrificed his life for the other?

Friedman was gritting his teeth. Grief had ambushed him again. He'd thought he'd done with tears, thought he'd drained himself dry by now, crying secretly in his bedroom at night, or that time was doing the healing stuff people went on about, but his eyes were stinging and there was a boulder in his throat. He'd thought that at least he wouldn't cry in public, that the memorial service wouldn't be as bad as the funeral where he'd wondered which bits of his dad were in the coffin, but now his chest felt as if it was splitting.

"Gave his life willingly..." intoned the chaplain.

Because he didn't think! Because he joined the military and let others think for him.

"To defend his country..."

Because he believed liars!

He watched three chins, his mother's and his grand-mothers' jut up proudly.

"God knows..." said the chaplain.

Then why doesn't He stop it?

At least the anger stopped the tears. Shut UP! Face the truth! He wanted to yell. It was a pointless waste! My father was duped! He fried in burning fuel. He exploded into little charred bits! He became a Fried Man!

At last it came to an end, and as his grandmothers took hold of the girls' hands he shot out of a side door.

Hilde watched Marty and the chaplain coming towards her down the aisle, followed by other front row mourners. But where was Friedman? She'd lost sight of him. Here came the girls holding – she guessed – their grandmothers' hands. But where had he gone? Other people were leaving their seats. Now there was a procession behind Marty who had nearly reached the back of the chapel. As she disappeared through the doors at the back Frank and Tom moved into the aisle, joining the back of the procession, and Hilde followed, hoping she'd see Friedman outside.

But as they stepped into the sunshine the queue slowed, then halted, and – she looked all around – there was still no sign of him. Marty and the chaplain were standing on a piece of ground covered with flowers, and people were filing past them, and not just filing past, but stopping to shake Marty's hand or kiss her cheek. Friedman's sisters and his grandmothers were looking at the flowers, but there was no sign of him. Had he gone? Didn't he want to see her? The queue shuffled forward. It was nearly their turn. Then it was their turn, and Marty was saying how she hoped they would come to the reception in the Officers' Social Club. Why didn't she just go home and howl, Hilde thought – and where was Friedman?

He had just arrived at the club, and was standing at a fruit machine, keeping an eye on the door, which he could see reflected in the shiny surface. After a bit, when people started to stream in from the chapel, he started to play to discourage anyone from coming over to talk. No one seemed to want to, thank God. Would she want to? Would she come or had what she heard back there made her throw up? He'd seen her, fleetingly, just before he'd walked out. Did she think he still believed that crap? If she did, she wouldn't come. Behind him people started to drink Cokes and beers and talk great guy and ball games. Cally and Olivia arrived with the old ladies, and started to run around the hall with two other little girls as if they hadn't a care in the world. That was OK. They'd cried enough. But his grandmothers, whom he'd never ever seen cry, were sitting together sipping iced tea. If either of them said, 'Be brave' meaning 'Kid yourself' one more time…

Then words froze in his head. The scene round him faded. The sound cut out. She was here. She'd come. Hilde, her hair like a golden halo, was standing in the doorway.

She saw him as soon as she walked through the door.

Frank and Tom carried on walking into the room which seemed to fade away. For a moment voices hung in the air. 'Great guy.' 'Terrible loss.' Then it was as if someone turned down the sound and all she could hear was her own heart pounding. All she could see was Friedman turning towards her. Then he was by her side, his hand cupping her elbow, steering her back through the door. 'Let's get away from these assholes.'

Threading their way through people still arriving, he led her away from the building, crossed the road, crossed another road, passed the High School and the Junior High, passed the playing fields, passed the motor pool and the dig-site, where he paused for a moment. A building site now, it stood silent and empty of people, surrounded by wire fences. Behind them stood the shell of a two-storey building. The new accommodation block? Surely he hadn't brought her to see this?

She glanced at him. "What..."

But he was off again with her in tow, willingly, but where, where was he taking her? To the war memorial? Somehow she thought not, though they were heading that way, and soon it was in front of them, shining white in the sunshine, the steps piled high with flowers, the flag flying high. But he turned left before they reached it, onto a path which led to a grassy area and now she guessed where they were going. She remembered her own moonlight visit the night she'd walked home from Pyghtle Cottage. The path led into trees, bordering a pond, and here they were. He stopped by a willow, pulled back the dangling branches and drew her into a shadowy cave.

Breathless, they looked through the leaves into the water, as if they dare not look at each other, saw their reflections floating, blurring and overlapping though they stood separate now. The inches between them felt like a chasm.

"*Crap*. I'm sorry you had to listen to that crap. But you were right. There must be satisfaction in that."

"No!"

"It was a *waste*."

"Saddam's gone..."

"No!" He turned and put his fingers on her lips. "Not you."

She tasted salt and wanted to drink him.

"Don't you, please, try and comfort me with shit. No lies. Let us at least be real. You were right. You understood."

She moved his hand from her lips but kept tight hold. "No lies?"

"No lies." They looked straight at – into – each other and she struggled to comfort him and tell the truth. "It isn't a simple choice between war bad and peace good. Saddam's regime wasn't peaceful. He killed hundreds of thousands of people because they disagreed with him. It isn't peace if you're afraid to speak the truth."

"But isn't truth the first casualty of war?"

"Yes – we've been lied to – but wouldn't your dad be glad he's gone?"

"Yet the killing goes on. It's madness. First we armed Saddam Hussein so he could kill thousands of people, then we turned on him killing thousands more. Now they're killing us again, and there's more terrorism all over the world. Osama bin Laden, who they know planned 9/11, is alive and well and his followers are all over the place, including Iraq. Bent on revenge, the USA didn't even go after the right man. You said the cure would be worse than the disease and you were more right than you knew. Now,' his voice dropped, 'I know. Thousands like me know. American, British, Iraqi, who cares? We've paid the price of war. Don't tell me, or them, that there isn't another way."

He turned away from her, to look into the water. She looked too and saw the water shimmer, saw her reflection ripple so her blue combats looked like a long blue dress and suddenly a dazzlingly clear picture was in her head, of Manfried and Maethilde, so clear she thought for a moment they might be standing in front of her, that it was their reflections floating in the water, overlapping, merging, but – she checked – there was no one else, just Friedman and herself, standing, perhaps, where they had once stood, listening to the wind whispering, thinking Wyrd was whispering to them. Weave. Weave. Word weave. Peace weave.

She took Friedman's hand.

"Manfried and Maethilde," she said when she could speak. "The Peace Weavers, they thought Wyrd wove the pattern of our lives, choosing the threads, crossing,

220

twisting and breaking them as she thought fit."

"And what do you think?"

"That we're given the threads and we choose what to do with them, and I think in a way they thought so too. They chose to be Peace Weavers and friends, loving friends, not the first perhaps..."

"And not the last..." He pulled her to him, loosened the scarf holding her hair, and his lips touched hers. At last. Closing her eyes, she felt his fingers in her hair, his heart beating against hers and wanted the moment to last forever.

But he pulled away – just a little away. "Was that... OK?"

She nodded. Couldn't speak. Why had he stopped?

"Peace weaving, it begins here, right?"

She nodded again, dumb again.

"And, as you said, now we've got to start spreading the word till everyone sees that it's the only way forward. People can, do change. I've thought about this a lot. Once slavery was normal. Decent people thought it was OK, just as decent people today think war is OK. But one day – it'll take time – but one day people will look back on our age in disbelief that we were so crass, that we spent so much on arms, that we used scarce resources to destroy. They'll think the twentieth century and the beginning of the twenty-first – but not I hope the end – were barbaric. Some people in the past made a start with peace weaving, but it's up to us, our generation, to work even harder, to make peace work..."

He stopped. She was staring at him. "You think I'm crazy?"

"No!" She pulled him to her.

"I didn't mean to make a speech."

"It was great. You be President. I'll run the UN. We'll work together. Peace weaving is an idea whose time has come, but this as you said is where it begins." She kissed him on the lips, lightly, not as he'd kissed her, but there would be time for that later.

"We'll be on opposite sides of the Atlantic for a bit."

"No problem. Seas have been crossed before."

And as she spoke the branches stirred and that dazzling picture was there again. Manfried and Maethilde were there again. She saw and felt they were there, urging them forward. Peace weave. Word weave. The branches stirred, the blue water rippled and the words of a poem were on her lips.

""The woods are lovely, dark, and deep.""

""But *we* have promises to keep."" Friedman knew it too.

""And miles to go before *we...*"" Jets blitzed the last word.

As F-15s screamed overhead, Friedman held Hilde close till the engines were a distant whine. Then he pulled back the branches and together they stepped towards the sunlight.

After Words

My story ended in the summer of 2003, with Hilde and Friedman dedicating their lives to peace. Today, as images of war still fill our TV screens and newspapers, they may seem crazily idealistic. Peace looks unattainable, war unstoppable. But it seems to me that Hilde and Friedman are right. They are the realists, because they know what war is really like.

The violence in Iraq has continued – despite the defeat and capture of Saddam Hussein – and it has spread to other countries across the globe. On July 7th 2005 suicide bombers killed fifty-two people in London, fifty-six if you include the bombers. Pictures of the massacre filled our screens. We were shocked and horrified – as we were meant to be – and perhaps forgot that a similar massacre is happening *every day* in Iraq. In July 2005 the bodies of 1,100 civilians were taken to the morgue in Baghdad. During the war no one counted the bodies of Iraqi people so we do not know how many died.

One thing is clear. Violence breeds violence. Revenge attack follows revenge attack.

So how will Hilde and Friedman become peace weavers? When I wrote the book I knew they would try to resolve disputes in their personal lives, but I didn't know how they would achieve their ambition to work for peace in the wider world. Now I do, because the publication of *Peace Weavers* has brought me into contact with hundreds of real-life peace weavers! In April I was invited to speak at the annual conference of the Peace Education Network. I learned that skilled people, trained to resolve and prevent conflicts, are operating all over the world – and even more exciting – that some of them are succeeding!

One example – the IRA was once as feared as Al Qaeda is now. Only a few years ago our newspapers and TV screens were filled with reports of their attacks. Gradually – it has taken years – skilled negotiators have brought the two sides in this dispute together. Slowly, terrorism has given way to talk, and now the future of Ireland will be decided by ballot not bullets.

Sadly, conflicts resolved and conflicts prevented don't make the front pages, but you can find out how and where this is happening. Read "War Prevention Works" by Dylan Mathews or "Unarmed Heroes" by Peace Direct, or log on to www.oxfordresearchgroup.org.uk, the website of an organisation dedicated to the prevention of war and the promotion of non-violent solutions to conflict.

I now think Hilde's next step after A Levels might be to study for a degree in Peace Studies at Bradford or Warwick or one of several universities who offer it. I think Friedman may well study Nuclear Physics with a view to working for an organisation like the Oxford

Research Group who employ scientists, military experts, weapons designers and government officials to develop ways to prevent war. Perhaps he will become a weapons inspector.

We now know that weapons inspectors who entered Iraq *after* the war didn't find any WMDs – the stated reason for going to war – and the search for weapons has now been called off. As the truth about the war emerges and the death toll rises public opinion is changing.

As I write, peace campaigners are gathered outside Camp David, President Bush's holiday home, protesting against the continued occupation of Iraq by American forces. Pro-war campaigners have joined them. The debate still goes on, but the number of peace campaigners has surged this year, which has also seen the launch of the campaign to Make Poverty History. The link is obvious. War is the biggest cause of poverty in the world. Poverty is a major cause of war. If we want to Make Poverty History we must stop war. If we want to stop war we must eradicate poverty *and peace weave*. It is common sense.

Spread the word!

Julia Jarman
August 2005